RAINE MILLER

writing as Brit DeMille

LUCKY
Puck

LUCKY
Puck

VEGAS
CRUSH

grant gerard

general manager

LUCKY
Puck

7

dedication

Coach G

You were first.

1
max terry

Grant

"So, it's done then, hey?" Marcus asks as he takes a swig from his beer bottle. "The i's are crossed and the t's are dotted?"

I open my mouth to respond but then realize what he's said. "I think you got that backward, friend."

He lifts a shoulder. "Whatever. You get the picture."

I nod. "Yep. I signed all the paperwork yesterday in the presence of my lackluster divorce attorney. We're selling the house and splitting the proceeds, but I might as well just hand her the money, considering all the spousal support I've had to pay to get to this point." I take a swig from my own bottle. "Just glad our financials are now and forever severed."

"Bitch cheats on you in your own bed and then asks you to pay her to go away," Marcus answers, shaking his head of wild, blond curls. "Did you at least get to punch Barton Graves in the face?"

I cringe at his choice of word. *Bitch.* I just don't like to talk about her like that. Even after she had an affair with one of my (former) best friends. Even after she acted as if our fourteen years spent together meant nothing. "I'm not paying her to go away and...don't call her that." I toy with the label on my beer.

"Dude, you're too nice. Too much of a gentleman. She did you wrong."

"She did," I agree. But I still don't like that word. For any woman, really."

He lifts his shoulder again. "Okay, man. Sorry. And what about Barton?"

"I've got nothing to say about Barton. He's nobody to me now."

"Gonna make work holiday parties a real hoot."

I snort at this. He's not wrong. The thought of having to be in a room together with the two of them, in front of the team and the whole office staff? No thanks. It curdles my stomach, actually. Makes my beer taste sour. "A shitshow indeed."

Marcus nods, his mouth set in a distasteful pucker. "With a capital *S*. I'll bet you wish you'd never heard the name Margot at this point."

Margot. We met when I was twenty-four, just two years out of college. I'd taken my college team to the national championships playing center, and there was no way I wasn't going to make a career of the game I'd been playing since I could stand in a pair of skates. I went straight into the AHL and made a name for myself early.

One night, my teammates and I were out celebrating. The usual group of hockey groupies were hanging around, eager to spend the night with a pro player. Any pro player. But that wasn't an interest of mine. However, my eyes did keep wandering to a table full of college-aged women, where a pretty blonde with blue eyes was trying very hard not to look as interested as I thought she might be.

I went to the restroom just to get a chance to walk by her table. We made eye contact, and when I came back out, I asked if I could buy her a drink. Margot and I were inseparable after that night. She was always in the stands, cheering for me. She watched my career take off, was there when I won the Calder Cup, and saw me represent my country as the Canadian team took Olympic Gold in Sochi.

And then.

And then that thing happens that all pro athletes dread. The injury that brings it all to a screeching halt. For me, it was my knee. Not your usual ACL or meniscus tear for me. No, I shattered my knee, a hard feat when you're covered in pads. Thank God for knee replacement surgery, but still, those manufactured joints are not made for pro athletes. After fifteen years of professional hockey, I was out. Hence, the move into management.

And I'm good at it. I like it. I had a lot of good years as a player, and now I'm a damn good administrator. So that's all fine.

However, I am an administrator at a team that, due to a prolific grapevine, now knows my wife cheated on me with my best friend and the CFO for the team. No *bueno*.

When did my marriage fall apart? Hard to know, which I guess means I wasn't a very attentive partner. I'd thought Margot was the one. I loved her. I thought she loved me back. That we were happy. I wanted kids. She wanted kids. We tried for years and never had luck. Every month, her period came like clockwork, and every month, I found myself disappointed. Frustrated. Because I always wanted a family. And I wanted it with her, so it felt like my failure when it never happened.

So here I am at thirty-nine, divorced, and replaying it all over and over as I try to figure out where I could have been better, done better, as a husband. My friends all think it wasn't me—that, really, it was Margot who disengaged. She's the one who cheated, that's true, but people don't cheat if things are great between them and their spouses.

Marcus nudges me out of my thoughts. "Hey, bro, your phone is buzzing. Come back to earth."

Blinking away my stroll down memory lane, I pick up my phone from the table. A Las Vegas number I don't recognize scrolls across the top of the screen. I consider letting it go to voicemail, but frankly, I could use some air, so I grab it and stand, heading for the door.

"This is Grant," I answer as I step out into the cool night.

"Hey, Grant," an unfamiliar voice says on the other end of the line. "Sorry to call you after hours. Is this a good time?"

"That depends. Are you trying to sell me something?"

A chuckle. "No. My name is Max Terry."

Max Terry. Max Terry. The name is so familiar, but I can't place it.

"I'm the owner of the Las Vegas Crush."

The fuck? The Las Vegas Crush, a top-five team in the NHL who've won the cup and eaten up a shit-ton of talent over the past few years. Whoa.

"Well, hello, Mr. Terry. How can I be of service?"

"Our long time GM has recently told me he intends to retire before the season starts. We're sad to see him go, obviously, but excited to bring in some new ideas. Fresh perspective. We need to move quickly, though, to get him replaced. I'm calling to see if you'd consider a conversation with us?"

He wants to know if I would *consider* a conversation with the Las Vegas Crush? About taking the top administrative role at a team that is literally at the very pinnacle of the NHL?

"I would definitely consider a conversation." I try

to keep the eagerness out of my voice. "But what made you think of me, sir?"

"I've heard good things. You're a former player with a ton of league awards under your belt. You're a Gold medalist. You're not a media liability. You've got good, solid management experience, from what I've heard. Young, fresher in your approaches. Well respected. I could go on, but I don't want to give you too big an ego boost."

"No worries, there. I just got hammered in a divorce settlement, so my ego is good and surely managed right now."

Why did I just tell him that?

Luckily, he laughs. "Boy, don't I understand that. But I'll tell you, it's good news for me. No baggage. It's a chance to come in fully focused on the team, and I really need that right now. I've got a roster full of amazing players with huge salaries. It's been a good run, but I have a real concern about our bench strength and our longevity. Come down for a visit, Grant, and we can talk more about it."

"Yes, of course. I work with Nic Marchessault at Talent One. Can your HR team liaison through him to set things up?"

"We can. We'll get ahold of your agent and get you down here posthaste."

"Sounds good. Looking forward to it."

"Grant, keep this under your hat. The team hasn't

been informed yet and we're only looking at a couple of guys. I want to keep it quiet for now."

"Roger that."

"Also, I may hire an assistant GM. We haven't had one here in a few years and I'd like to get with the diversity bandwagon. You aren't a racist or a sexist, right? Because I'm looking at a couple of women for the role."

"No, sir. I'll work with anyone with a brain for hockey and a desire to be a team player."

"Good man. See you soon."

He hangs up, and I stand there for a long minute, taking in what just happened. When I finally make my way back inside to the bar, Marcus has ordered another round. I reach for the bottle and take an extra-long pull before meeting my friend's inquisitive gaze. "Guess who that was."

"Your attorney?"

"No."

"Margot?"

"No. Thank God."

"I give up."

"That, my friend, was the owner of a major NHL team. Things might just be looking up after all."

Talk about incredible timing. This could be the perfect opportunity to put the shitshow in Alberta behind me and discard all the "baggage" attached to it. And I can move forward with my life.

2
the full conference experience

Devon

"What is this, Grandma's first FaceTime?" Gia asks as I fumble to turn the camera around on my phone.

"Shut up, you know I'm not a huge techie." Giggling, I get the screen pointed away from my face and at the spacious hotel room I'm in. "Voila! There we go."

Gia rolls her eyes into my phone screen. "Give the girl a medal."

"Look at this room! It's so pretty. And the view is amazing," I gush, walking around to show her the space.

"I'll agree it does look swanky. However, you are maybe the most boring person I know. You live here, Devon. All of Vegas is your home. So why would you get a hotel room in your own city? You live like fifteen minutes from that hotel."

"I'm having the full conference experience. Just because I live here doesn't mean I should miss out on the experience I would've had if the Sports Nutrition Expo was in, say, New York City."

"Okie dokie." Gia sounds dubious and obviously amused. "I'm just saying, you could've saved seven hundred bucks and gotten a flight to Mexico this summer instead. You could've taken your good friend and neighbor with you, and we both could have had fun in a place that is not in our backyard."

"It's fun," I say, pushing my lips out in a pout. "Don't poop on my parade."

Gia giggles uncontrollably at this. "Don't poop on your parade?"

"You're a mean person."

"I'm not. But you have to admit that you're dipping a toe into boring old lady territory, if your idea of fun is getting a hotel room at a work conference in your own town."

"I do fun things. There's a spa here at the hotel. I could get a massage or a facial. Maybe a mani-pedi."

Gia closes her eyes and snores in response.

"I get to work with pro athletes every day," I snap. "That's exciting enough."

"Dude, I'd have a *way* more exciting life than you if *I* worked around all those hotties all day long."

"Well, then you'd be fired, because you sign a non-fraternization agreement when you go to work for the

Vegas Crush Organization. It'd be a lot less exciting not having a paycheck, too."

"The Vegas Crush Organization is clearly miscommunicating that message, then. Didn't you tell me that there's been like five marriages between players and staff recently? The whole freaking world knows about the Crush goalie, Cal Lefleur, and Billie Hirsch getting engaged a few months back."

"Yes, but Cal and Billie weren't bound by that policy as she didn't work for the Crush. Only three actual marriages...to date...that would be in direct violation of the non-fraternization rule. A couple of engagements still planning their big day, but again, if the fiancée is not an employee of VCO, your point is moot."

"Still. Clearly there's some old-fashioned fraternizin' goin' on up in there, if you know what I'm saying." Her tone and facial expression tell me she'd be elbowing me in the ribs if we were together in person.

"Maybe, but that's not for me. You know I married a basketball player far too young and the four years we spent together taught me that I am not in the market for a pro athlete. They are just big boys, and I need a man."

"That I can get behind," Gia says. "How is ole Shawn these days?"

"I don't know. He's playing in Miami and I'm thankful to be on the other side of the country."

"Is he still with the woman he cheated on you with?"

"Of course not. He told me marriage wasn't what he wanted. He felt like we got married too young and he wanted to sow his oats or whatever. So he's out doing that, I guess."

"Yuck."

"No doubt. But he's not wrong. I was a freshman in college when we met and a sophomore when we got married. That's too young."

"It actually surprises me that you would make such a spontaneous decision," Gia says.

"I was in love, and he was the big man on campus. He was getting NBA recruiters out to see him all the time, so it was only a matter of time for him to get picked up to play pro. And at twenty, I thought being married to a pro basketball player would be glamourous and romantic."

"Well, he's a shit for breaking your heart."

"He says that from time to time." I let out a sigh. "It's okay. We're mostly cool now and he's living his best life or whatever. I've just learned to guard myself, you know?"

"Well, don't guard yourself for too long. You're, like, the most beautiful woman in the world and a damn fine catch. I'd hate to see you miss out on someone good."

"Are you trying to get rid of me?"

Gia laughs. "No, definitely not. But I'd at least like

to see you take a booty call every once in a while. A girl's gotta get off."

"Who says I don't?"

"With a person. Not a vibrating massager that they keep stashed in their nightstand drawer."

"How do you know what's in my nightstand drawer?"

She makes a face and changes the subject. "So what's on the docket for your oh-so-exciting sports nutrition conference?"

"Well, there's a product expo, and a keynote by this top sports doc that wrote the best book about…"

I'm interrupted by the sound of snoring again.

"And there's a mixer tonight in the bar," I say drily.

Gia perks up at this. "Okay, that's promising."

"Well, I wasn't gonna go because I was planning on taking a long bubble bath, ordering expensive room service, and watching Netflix in this big-ass bed."

My friend is silent, but her raised eyebrow says enough.

"I mean…I guess I could go, but do you want to come down and go with me?"

"Okay, you big introvert. I'll come protect you from the legions of people who will try to say actual words to you."

I have to laugh because I am, indeed, an introvert. I'd absolutely rather take a bath and curl up with a good book or binge-watch a show. The idea of mixing and mingling with people I don't know, keeping a smile plastered to my face while I ask, "What do you do?" forty different times just doesn't sound all that fun to me.

AN HOUR LATER, Gia knocks on my door. Dressed to kill in a short, black skirt and cheetah-print top, she's obviously not impressed by my choice of business suit, from the way her lip curls as she looks me over from head to toe.

"You are eighty years old, I swear," she scolds, shaking her head and clucking her tongue.

"What? It's a professional conference, not a nightclub. These are other nutritionists."

"It's a mixer," she insists. "In a bar. Wear a pair of jeans, you old woman, you."

I look helplessly at my closet. I brought lots of options because it's been a while since I've been to a multi-day conference like this. Gia just huffs and stomps over, rifling through my clothing until she emerges, triumphant, with a pair of skinny jeans and a soft, off-the-shoulder, cream-colored sweater. "These will do. You got heels?"

"I do." I grab the outfit and head into the bathroom to change.

Gia has me sit while she styles my long, brown hair into a messy bun, telling me it makes my neck look sexy when I wear my hair up. I pull on a pair of nude peep-toe heels, and she declares me "perfecto," while kissing her fingertips.

I keep my makeup simple, just eyeliner and mascara and a light-pink lip gloss because that's pretty much how I roll on a normal day.

I present myself to my friend, holding my hands up for her honest assessment.

Gia gives me a thumbs-up, grabs me by the hand, and proceeds to practically drag me from the safety of my room.

I'm pretty sure the "full conference experience" I wanted is about to get painfully real.

3
really rusty

Grant

I loosen my tie while making my way down the hall to my room, finally allowing myself a full breath.

I am now the new general manager of the Las Vegas Crush.

I'm the new GM of the fucking Vegas Crush.

Two weeks ago, I'd have laughed at you in the face if you said I'd be moving to the States to run an NHL team. But here I am, having just accepted a rather lucrative deal to take over a team that is full of superstars and within the immediate sphere of the Cup for the third time in four years.

Holy shit. How did this happen?

I pull off my tie and flip open my laptop, sending a video call through to my parents, who are waiting anxiously for an update. My dad's face appears first, then my mom's.

"So?" my dad asks without preamble.

"I won two hundred bucks at blackjack?"

My dad rolls his eyes as my mom scolds, "Stop that. What happened in your interview?"

"You are looking at the new GM for the two-time NHL champion, Las Vegas Crush."

Mom cheers, and Dad gives me the half-smile that tells me he's proud of me. "Did you talk to Nic about it first? Get the best deal?"

"I spent two hours with the owner, an hour with the head coach, and then we spent two hours on the phone with Nic while we hammered out a deal."

"Good man. Go get a drink to celebrate."

"Las Vegas has a bit of a reputation," my mom warns. "Just be careful not to call attention to yourself before you even get started there."

"Have you met me?" I'm grinning. "I'm not exactly the run-the-city type. I'll just have some dinner in my room and hit the hay, I think. It was a long day."

"No, no," Dad says, shaking his head. "Grant. It's a dream job in an amazing city. Go out and enjoy it. See what it feels like. Maybe take in a show or something."

I definitely won't be taking in a show, but I don't tell him that. Instead, we talk about the deal a little more before saying good night, but by the end of our call, I decide I'll at least go down to the hotel bar. I'll get a steak and a couple fingers of whisky and that'll be celebration enough for me.

Unbuttoning the top button of my shirt, I decide

not to change out of my suit pants and jacket to save time since I'll be celebrating alone. Heading back out to the elevator and down to the concierge level, there are a ton of people at the bar, so I change course for the restaurant and ask for a table.

"Why so many people in the bar?" I ask, eyeing the crowd.

The hostess seats me with a view of the bar, saying, "There's a conference here all week. They're having a mixer."

I take my seat, ordering my celebratory Macallan as I peruse the menu. Once my server returns with my drink, I order their signature porterhouse and scroll through my phone, checking emails and finding the initial paperwork for my new role already awaiting my review.

Scanning quickly, I realize I'll need to pull this contract up on my laptop later, so I close down my phone and look up at the mingling crowd in the bar. It's one of those awkward, professional networking things. People holding their wine glasses, smiling and nodding, trying to connect on a level that is professionally distant. My eye catches on a petite woman near the end of the bar. Some kind of light club music is playing, and she's dancing along, clearly uninterested in the crowd around her. It's silly, really, but then I figure out she's purposely trying to annoy the person she's with.

The person she's with.

The stunning creature proceeds to turn away from her dancing friend, holding out her hand to stop the ridiculous bump and grind from continuing.

Her smile is infectious, and—I—I feel like I've hit a ten-foot fuckin' brick wall. The beating of my heart just definitely stuttered, went offline for a second before sputtering back into its normal rhythm.

I felt that shit happen in real time.

She might be the most beautiful woman I have ever seen in person. Ever. In my life. Tall and willowy, her dark hair piled on top of her head, exposing an elegant neck I indecently imagine the fantasy of kissing. I have to forcibly keep myself from staring.

I don't think anyone has ever stopped me in my tracks like she just did. In fact, I know nobody has.

Try as I might to push my thoughts elsewhere; I do not. Instead, I steal glances in between sips of my Macallan, drinking in her creamy skin, the perfect profile, and the length of her legs in slim jeans.

The flash of a thought to get up and go talk to her and introduce myself comes to mind, but when the server returns with my meal, I settle back into my chair.

What's the point? I'm moving here soon. She's probably just here for this conference. Our orbits are crossing but likely only for this one space in time. And frankly, I'm just out of a marriage that went down in flames, so I don't think I'm up for any kind of thing, even in the short-term. *Even for one night.* Man, am I jaded. I can only hope Margot's betrayal doesn't shape me forever. I am a man who loves sex. But it's been part of a committed, *faithful* marriage for the last fourteen years. Seems that's hard to shake.

As I eat my steak and drink my whisky, I watch Crush highlights on my phone. They're good. Organized. They have good chemistry, and they have a natural pass that speaks to team unity and trust. It's a good vibe, at least among their first-string players. From my interview conversations, I gather they're worried about what happens if one of those superstars retires or gets hurt. They play second- and third-string players but not often and not for more than a few minutes at a time. This team relies on those heroes, and the rest are pretty much untested.

That needs to change.

Frankly, I'm surprised they haven't had an uprising from the bench. Guys don't join pro teams just to sit on the bench. But I also get the coaching team's nerves around upsetting the apple cart. They have a good thing going. Why fix what isn't broken?

I sneak a few more peeks at the bar area, at one point catching the eye of the beauty standing there, a soft, cream sweater hanging off her bare shoulder. She holds my gaze for a heartbeat before looking away, a small act that makes my heart speed up its thumping inside my chest.

Once I'm finished, the server comes to take my plate, asking if I want dessert. I decline and she sets the bill down. As I sign for the meal, I catch the woman's eye again. This time, she holds my gaze. She doesn't blush or demure, but instead gives me a soft smile before turning back to her friend.

I'm officially intrigued as I drain the last of my whisky. She looks like the kind of woman who attracts attention, and the soft smile wasn't indifferent, but it wasn't flirtatious or salacious at all, either. She may be ambivalent to male attention if she gets hit on a lot. Maybe she's perfected a polite smile to combat any unwanted attention.

Frankly, it's been so long since I've had to think about my game with the ladies I feel like a bit of an oaf.

I'm *really* rusty.

Do I chance it and go say hello? Do I chalk it up as a loss and head back to my room? I'm a thirty-nine-year-old man in a fourteen-year-old's head all of a sudden.

As I stand, I think I've decided to just go back to my room and call it an early night, but every step I take brings me closer to this incredible beauty.

And when she turns and meets my gaze once more?

I decide one more drink might not hurt at all.

4
ask me anything

Oh God. That hot guy is coming this way.

Broad shoulders fill out his jacket with the suggestion of strong muscles moving underneath. He's tall, at least six five, with dark hair and a slight five-o'clock shadow. He's in a suit that fits really, *really* well, his crisp, white shirt open at the throat. No tie. He looks smart and professional and slick. Like, if he came to my house to sell me a vacuum cleaner, I'd probably buy two.

I turn to Gia, my face clearly set to Full Panic. "It's fine, Dev. He'll probably ask to buy you a drink. It will be good." She nods slowly at me with a teasing grin.

"Anything in my teeth?" Before she can answer, I add, "My hair look okay?"

Gia snickers. "You're perfect."

"How's my breath?" I ask, blowing in her face.

"Fine. Jesus, Devon, I've never seen you so twisted up about a random...oh, here he is."

I turn to find the super-hot guy is even hotter up close. Warm hazel eyes, movie-star face. My panties melt a little.

"Hi," he says.

My throat is suddenly totally dry. I mean, I am *thirsty*. I smile, but I'm pretty sure I might look like I'm in pain. Somehow, I squeak out a, "Hey."

Gia adds to my misery by looking at her nonexistent watch and saying, "Oh, geesh, look at the time. I've got a thing to check in on. Have a good night and call me later."

And she *leaves*. My wretched, wretched little beast of a best friend leaves me all alone with this gorgeous man. A man so gorgeous, in fact, I think he could give micro-orgasms by looking at me like he's doing right now. *Wow.*

"Can I join you for a drink?" He gestures to where two seats have magically opened at the bar.

I bite my lip and nod, and it's the darndest thing— he gives me an honest to God, authentic smile. It feels like a real smile, as if he's relieved. Like he thought I might say no and he's genuinely happy I said yes. I can barely find my own tongue in my mouth right now, so it's hard to believe this guy would ever be worried about any woman saying no, but still...it makes me feel oddly special.

It's disarming.

He looms for a moment, leaning over the bar to catch the bartender's attention. He's got to be six five, six six. Very tall. Very broad. Athletic. So very vibrator-worthy. *I'll be remembering him when I bust it out of my suitcase later.*

We place our drink orders, and as the bartender walks away, he says, "So you're here for a conference, I gather?"

I nod. "The forced small talk gave it away, or what?"

"The name badges, mostly," he says, grinning. "Though you seem to have forgotten yours."

I look down and realize I have, indeed, forgotten my name badge. "Oops."

Our drinks come and we each take a sip before I ask, "I take it you are not here for a conference?"

"No, a job interview." He strokes his chin with his thumb and index finger until they meet in the middle. *Oh, Lord, help me.*

"Oh—oh, where are *you* from?" I cringe internally at my stammer.

"Alberta." Ah, that explains the very slight accent I hear in his voice. *He's Canadian. A really hot, sexy Canadian.*

"And what do you think of Vegas so far?"

He lifts a shoulder. "So far, it's been good. I haven't seen much of it, though I do like what I've seen very much."

The comment comes along with a look that tells

me he is not talking about the city. And it makes me extremely uncomfortable between the legs.

He seems to be eating up the sight of my squirming, the tiniest smirk playing at his lips as I squeeze my crossed legs together to stop the heated desire that pools there. *Did it just get really hot in here?*

Yes! Why yes, it did.

I think I need a glass of water. And a cold pool to jump in.

"So, I'm wondering if you'd be up for a challenge," he says smoothly.

"Oh?"

"I'm thinking we could try talking about anything other than our jobs or old relationships."

"I suppose we could give it a try. Though I do work a lot, so it might be hard."

"I'll bet you're much more than your job. You start. Ask me anything."

I look at him through narrowed eyes as I think of a question. "What kind of music do you like?"

He sits back on his bar stool, his glass of whisky in hand. "I like lots of different types of music, honestly. I listen to rock music to pump myself up. I like country music when I'm having my feels. Rap music is fun when I'm driving. I hate musicals, though. Hope that's not a deal breaker?"

"No, it's not. I love theater, and I love dance, and I love music, but put them all together and I suddenly want to throw myself in front of a speeding train."

"My kind of woman," he says, that grin of his killing me all over again. "My turn. What is your favorite vegetable, and which one turns your stomach?"

"Well, I love to cook, so I'm not that picky, honestly. I love transforming greens into something unique, so I guess they're my favorite? They don't turn my stomach, but I'm not a huge fan of mushrooms. If prepared right, I can tolerate them, but I don't relish the idea of eating fungus."

"Fair enough. Also not a fan of the mushrooms," he says.

"Okay...are you a dog or a cat person?"

"Um, both? I like animals. I don't have any pets, but I've thought about getting one recently. I'd probably get a cat because they seem more independent. I've always traveled a lot, and I feel like that wouldn't be fair to a dog, but a cat wouldn't care."

"I can see that. Your turn."

"Have you ever traveled abroad? What was your favorite place?"

"I have," I say. I almost say that my ex-husband made some international basketball trips but then stop myself, since talking about exes is off the table for this particular conversation. I take a sip of my cosmo and add, "I loved Italy. It was a breathtakingly beautiful country. The people are warm and passionate. The food is amazing. I think I gained ten pounds while I was there."

He points to my nearly empty glass with a questioning look, and I nod. "Maybe one more?"

Once our second round of drinks arrives, we resume our back-and-forth.

"Your turn," he prompts.

"Um...Mac or PC?"

This makes him laugh and I nearly lose it. Deep and sexy, it rumbles straight through me to land in my lower belly. I cannot with this guy, seriously. Such a sexy, sexy man, I might want to climb onto his lap like right freaking now.

I need to be honest with myself though. I am not drunk. I've had two and a half cosmos, and I can handle my liquor. And I do date sometimes, but most guys don't hold my interest. And I don't usually want someone in my bed the minute I meet them. In fact, most never make it that far, even after a few dates. This guy, though? I want him, and I'm not all that conflicted about it, either.

"Mac," he says, nodding. "I use an iPhone and I like having things sync. I think I've forgotten how to use Windows."

"That Apple does make a good product."

"What is your favorite sport?" he asks.

"To play or to watch?"

"Either. Both."

"Well, I like hockey to watch. And soccer. I played soccer in high school but then I got really into cross-country and track. I ended up running for two years in college, but then I got bored with the competition, and now I just run to stay healthy."

His eyebrows raise and I can't quite figure out what has surprised him. He just says, "Most people don't give up on college sports unless they have an injury."

I lift a shoulder. "I'm not a particularly competitive person. I just liked running, and I was good at it, and I got pulled into collegiate sports because it helped pay for school. But in the end, I just wasn't that excited about it. So...my turn?"

He nods. "Your turn."

We keep this up through the ends of our drinks, which takes a while. Maybe we're both enjoying this too much to rush? Possibly? I'm not totally sure of his take on this meeting, of course, but it feels like we have an easy connection.

He asks if I want another, but I err on the side of not wanting to be hung over in my conference sessions tomorrow. He refuses to let me pay for anything, and as we stand, our eyes meet, and he says, "I really want to kiss you right now. Is that weird? Would that be weird?"

My mouth hangs open. We're in the middle of a hotel bar and I don't know what I was expecting because I've been thinking about sex with him since, like, two minutes after we met, but still. I'm not a kiss-a-stranger-in-public kind of person.

When he asks, "May I?"

I nod.

He leans in and his lips are perfect against mine. He's not hesitant, but he's also not greedy. He's commanding, firm, his tongue grazes my bottom lip, and I melt into him, opening, letting him taste my mouth. He tastes like whisky and it's a heady thing. Literally intoxicating. His hand finds my lower back as he increases the intensity. I'm wet and throbbing, and it takes everything I have not to rub myself against him right here, in front of everyone in this bar.

When he pulls away, he looks as dazed as I feel. We stare at each other as I bite my lower lip again, contemplating what happens next.

I hear myself asking, "Is there more where that came from?"

It doesn't sound like my voice at all. In fact, I've never propositioned a guy before. *How did this happen?*

"My room or yours?" is his response.

5
living my best life

Grant

est day ever, I think as I hold this beautiful woman's hand, our pace frenzied as we head out of the bar toward the elevators. She swipes her room key and chooses her floor, and we stand hand in hand, nervous energy palpable in our silence.

When we step off, a cheerful *ding* rings through the air, and there's only the tiniest hesitation in her step before I'm towed along down the long hallway of gaudy carpet and poor lighting. Her steps are sure, her stride long. I take all of her in as we walk—the feminine shape of her ass in those jeans, the way her hair escapes her wild bun, the length of her neck, the peek of skin where her sweater drops from her shoulder.

Surely kissing her was as lucky as I will get. Surely

just seeing her, knowing a creature like her walks among us should be enough for me. Right?

We arrive at her room, and she swipes us in, the door closing with a heavy click behind us. We stare at each other hotly for a beat or two before she is on me. It's an attack unlike any I've ever experienced. Her lips are kissing mine. Her hands are in my hair. Her body presses against mine as my cock strains to greet her through the silk of my slacks.

She pushes my jacket off my shoulders, and my cock throbs at the thought of the unreal promise of what's to come.

Fuck.

This beautiful, lovely creature.

As my jacket falls to the floor, her busy fingers start to work on the buttons of my shirt. Four buttons are opened before her mouth moves—an undisputable eon of time before her lips drop down to kiss my chest. As her hands spread apart my shirt, her tongue licks over my pecs, my collarbone, both of my nipples.

It all feels so fucking good I get lost in the experience of being touched, kissed, licked— intimately. It's been so long since I've felt...

She breaks only long enough for me to pull my shirt over my head in an effort to assist in this process of getting naked.

She lets out a breathy sigh as I bare my torso. "God, I knew you'd be super ripped," she says, more to herself than to me.

I pull her to me, our lips meeting again as I pick her up, my hands on her ass, her legs wrapping around me as I walk toward the king-sized bed that's been placed on a platform near a bank of floor-to-ceiling windows. The amazing view of Vegas at night catches my attention only momentarily, a pale comparison to the woman in front of me.

I drop her onto the fluffy, white duvet, nipping at her lips, her ear, and that long elegant neck I fantasied about earlier down at the bar. She works my belt loose, then she unzips my pants. I toe off my shoes and kick them away as two thuds follow their path to somewhere on the floor. Then it's time to do the awkward shimmy out of my pants from a prone position on the bed, but I'm up for it.

So up for it.

Left only in my black boxer briefs, she pushes her hand down slowly beneath the fabric and wraps it around my cock, now fully hard and aching. *Holy. Fuck. So good.* My hips move in rhythm with her strokes as our tongues mingle, soft sighs and moans erupting from both of our throats.

"You're still dressed," I tell her, my voice more of a growl than anything else.

She lets out a little laugh and sits up, pulling her soft sweater over her head, her bun coming loose. One tug at the band that holds it in place and her long, soft, dark hair falls over her shoulders. I nearly lose it right there, she's so sexy. I move in quickly, pushing one breast out of the confines of a pale-yellow satin bra, my tongue and teeth grazing the bud of her nipple as it hardens beautifully beneath my mouth. Her response only makes my cock harder, if that's even possible.

My hands tug at her jeans as she kicks off her heels. They make softer thuds when they hit the floor than my shoes did a moment ago. The sounds of our clothes and shoes being hastily discarded cranks up the sensuality of the moment, electrifying the space between us, creating metaphorical arcs of high voltage. I swear my ears are buzzing.

Finally, she shimmies free of the last of the denim with a series of more helpful tugs from me. I toss those fuckin' jeans across the room where they land someplace, the metal button scraping over a surface before falling silent.

She laughs again, but I'm not sure at what. The sound of her jeans sliding down the wall? At me? At my eagerness to get her naked?

I don't really care at this point; I'm too far gone with lust to consider much of anything else but getting inside her.

Spreading her legs wide with my hands, my head moves down to kiss through the matching pale-yellow strip of satin covering her pussy. She moans, arching her back to create friction as her hands bury themselves in my hair again. Encouraged, I pull those little yellow panties down over her slim hips to join the rest of our discarded clothing, nearly drooling at the sight of her bare pussy lips framing a clit wet with arousal. *So deliciously wet.*

"Please," she begs, pushing her hips up. "Please."

I flick that slippery nub with my tongue, relishing the satisfied noise she makes and taste of her. My fingers work at her entrance, slipping inside. "You're so wet," I murmur, encouraged by the noises she makes, by the way her hips move to meet every flick of my tongue, every thrust of my fingers.

Suddenly, an almost panicked thought flies into my head. It comes out as fast as it came to me. "I—I just realized I don't know your name."

I say this with my mouth hovering above her most private of places, my fingers still moving inside of her. Looking up, I see she's looking at me, her dark eyes glittering, her shoulders shaking with laughter. "Well, look at us," she says through more laughter. "Living up to the stories about Vegas."

Grinning, I say, "Well, I'm Grant."

"Devon. And you look like a Grant. Like a movie star."

It's dark in the room but for the city lights outside the windows. Enough light that I can see her cheeks darken after she makes the comment. *She's embarrassed?* Fuck me, I'm the one who should be blushing. I'm just some big oaf with marginally good genes. This woman? She's a goddess. One I'm happy to bow to at the moment.

"I may be a bit tipsy," she says, biting her lip, still embarrassed for whatever unknown reason.

This stops me as understanding dawns. *That's why she's been laughing.*

I pull away from her and stand, putting my hand in hers and pulling her to a sitting position. Her hair is wild, her nipples overflowing the top of her bra. I may lose it in the next minute just looking at her like this. But still, I need to be sure this is okay.

"Are you sure you want this?" I ask. "We had some drinks, and I don't want you to regret this in the morning. I want to make sure you want it."

"You're sweet," she says, that blush spreading over her cheeks again. "But I think I'd regret *not* doing it. I mean...have you *seen* you? Have you looked in a mirror lately?"

I lean forward, hands on the bed on either side of her hips, lips hovering close to hers. "Have you?"

The noise Devon makes is guttural. Sexual. Frustrated. Full of want. And it makes me hard all over again. She leans forward, her lips on mine, her hand again on my cock, her tongue in my mouth.

I want to experience all of this woman's body so badly. If this is a one-night stand, then I aim to make it the best. I kiss along her jaw and neck as my fingertips pluck at her nipples, hard pearls in the cool, dry air of the hotel room. I suck and nip and she moans her approval, asking me for more, begging to make her come. My fingers slip back inside her hot, wet pussy, and she says, "Please," again in that breathless voice that urges me to pick up the pace. My mouth works at her perfect breasts while my fingers fuck her until her pussy quivers and clenches, her cry of satisfaction nearly enough to make me explode as I ride the wave, fingering her until she quiets, her breathing heavy, her eyes closed, a small, satisfied smile playing at her lips.

"I hate to step away from this, but give me a moment to grab a condom?"

She nods, still blissful, and I find my pants where they landed between the wall and the side of the bed, thankful that Marcus made me come here prepared. *Hey, Grant, it's Vegas; you never know.* And I'd laughed at him, thoroughly certain there was negative chance I'd be having sex with anyone while here for a job interview.

Working it over my cock, I make my way back to the bed. I lean in to kiss Devon. "This still okay?"

"Mm-hmm," she moans, reaching out to guide me into place. I'm a big guy, so it takes some maneuvering, but once I'm in...

We both moan at the same time, our bodies fitting so well together. Her hands find my ass as she leads me to move. Fingernails rake along my back as I start to thrust in and out, my mouth on her mouth, on her neck, on her perfect tits as she arches to push them toward me. The chemistry between us is intense but in only the best way.

I roll us over, placing her on top, and she moves her hips as I tease her erect nipples and run my hands over her creamy, soft skin. She comes again, her pussy clenching my cock as she throws her head back with a long moan. She stills as the wave of pleasure overtakes her, her skin erupting in gooseflesh, her hair hanging long down her back. I've never seen anything sexier in my whole life.

As her orgasm subsides—a minute, an hour, a lifetime, it seems to take—she says, "I want you."

"You have me," I say, but I know what she's asking for. We fit that well, and we both know it.

I help her off my hips and spread her out on the bed before me, moving her where I want her. I take her hands and curl them over the top of the headboard, setting them in place with a tap so her long, lean body is on display for me.

Our eyes meet in silent communication of understanding. She knows I want her in this position. I start at her feet and kiss my way up her inner thighs first, then her slick pussy, taking slow licks up and down her clit until she's writhing against my mouth. I say goodbye to her pussy and move on up over her stomach, across her hip, and up higher to kiss her even more spectacular breasts now that they're free of the bra. The final destination is my lips at her neck when I push back inside her, filling her all the way to my balls.

She nearly folds herself in two at my invasion,

pulling her legs up, allowing me to push even deeper inside of her. *So deep.*

Our eyes meet again, and once more, the connection is intense between us. Neither of us looks away. No one else in the world exists right now but the two of us sharing our bodies in the most carnal of ways.

Hell, nothing else in the world exists right now but the two of us fucking. Please, never let it end.

My pace intensifies with each subsequent thrust—as deep as I can sink my cock into her—over and over and over again.

Devon starts to shake, baring her teeth at me when she comes a third time, clenching hot and tight around my cock, her soft cries of pleasure triggering my own release. I allow myself to ride the wave this time, erupting hard and hot, literally seeing stars as intense pleasure overtakes everything else in the fucking world.

Devon's eyes lock with mine once more as I'm coming, linking us through sight and the sound of the pounding slides of my dick, fucking the last of its will into her. We simply cannot look away from each other. It's too exceptional our physical connection at this moment. My arms are literally spasming from holding me up, so I won't crush her. She shudders in pleasure beneath me, her dark eyes still locked on mine when I empty everything I've got deep inside her beautiful, willing body.

BREATHING HARD IN THE DARK, our bodies entangled, both of us coming down from the incredible high of the best sex *I* can ever remember—I nearly forgot that earlier today I was offered my dream job.

Paired with tonight, and the lovely woman in my arms after what we just did together?

I'd have to say...this is me living my best life. *Looks like I'm not irrevocably broken after all.*

6
fly as hell

Devon

I trace my fingers across Grant's muscular chest and then trail down farther to rest my hand low on his belly. He's stroking gently along the length of my arm. I'm boneless, totally unable to think or speak or move after what was, undoubtedly, the best sexual experience of my life.

The room is quiet but for the distant sounds of cars honking on the street below. I listen to the steady thump of his heartbeat for a long time, until the sound of my rumbling stomach jolts me back to the present. I guess I never really ate dinner.

"Hungry?" Grant asks.

"Famished, actually," I admit. "I ate some finger foods at that reception down in the bar but nothing of substance."

"Well," he grunts, extricating his thigh from

beneath my leg bent on top of it, "let me clean up and then I'll order us a snack, yeah?"

"That sounds good."

I have to fight to keep my eyes open; the war between hunger and sleep in a raging battle inside of me. I check the bedside clock, and it's nearly one in the morning. I need to get up and do a quick workout before breakfast. Maybe I should thank him and just say good night?

This new war rages in my head for what seems like a really long time. I'm not a one-night stand kind of person. I date, but not often. I have sex, but even less often, and definitely not with men I've just met in a bar. But something about Grant felt right to me. The chemistry was there when we first started talking, and the sex was hotter than hot. But should I tell him to go? Should I just end it here, send him on his way, and enjoy it for what it is? If he stays longer, it's likely I'll learn more about him. Perhaps I'll be sad to see him leave. Or perhaps he'll say something I hate and make me regret the whole thing.

I know I'm overanalyzing, and I can literally hear Gia's voice in my head, telling me to cut it out, to just go with the flow. Speaking of which, I should probably text her...

Tell him good night. End it here. Leave it casual and light. No need to make it more than it is. I can wait until breakfast to eat, and I'll be able to get a little more sleep for the conference.

My stomach grumbles angrily in response, and when Grant emerges, naked and cut like a stone statue, I forget all about my plan and my tiredness and my overanalyzing brain for a moment. It's suddenly important to me that I take in every inch of the sight of this man and commit it to memory. He is, by all accounts, the most beautiful man I have ever seen naked. This night and gorgeous Grant will be vibrator inspiration for a long time to come, I think. *I know.*

Grant looks at me for a moment, and there's something strange about his expression. He looks... conflicted, for lack of a better word. I hope I didn't break him. Before I can ask if everything is okay, he picks up the hotel phone and orders room service. When he turns back to me, the strange expression is gone. He pokes around at the various clothing items strewn about and finds his boxer briefs, slipping them on before sliding onto the bed next to me.

"You ordered a lot of fried nonsense there, friend," I say jovially.

"Post-alcohol food, Devon. Bad habit from my college days. Whisky does a thing to my taste buds. Makes me want junk."

"Blame it on the whisky, okay." I wink at him. "I don't usually eat stuff like that."

"Oh." He cringes. "Should I order something else?"

"No, no. It won't kill me to eat it one night. Live a little, and all. I'll work it off at the gym in the morning."

Grant peers at the bedside clock. "It is morning, kind of." His fingers trail along my still-bare body, dipping in between my legs and setting me instantly on fire. "And we could work it off now, ahead of time."

We kiss again, and he dips his fingers deeper inside me, stroking deep, while his thumb strums at my clit. I grasp his hardening cock beneath his boxers and we get right to work bringing each other to climax once again. We are so in sync it's like we've done this before...or something. Like the whole experience of being intimate together didn't require the usual groundwork before getting us to this point. It's strange, but yet, not unexpected...

GRANT LAUGHS as he rolls to his back. "I feel like a horny teenager. What are you doing to me, woman?"

A knock at the door startles us both, and now I'm the one laughing as he runs to the bathroom, wraps himself in a bath towel, and answers the door. He returns with a platter of food, placing the whole thing on top of the bed. I find my sweater within arm's reach and pull it over my head as Grant switches on the bedside lamp, filling the room with soft light.

"So you like to work out?" he asks, picking up a mozzarella stick and shoving it into his mouth. He makes a face as he chews and then says, "Shit. Hot."

I giggle and opt for a carrot and some hummus. "I

do. I do the gym maybe twice a week and I run maybe three days a week. Nothing crazy. I'm not like one of those CrossFit junkies or anything."

"How do you know someone does CrossFit?" Grant asks.

"They tell you," I finish.

We both laugh, and he says, "Though serious runners like to talk running, too. And cyclists. They can talk cycling all damn day."

"True stories, all of those. I've been known to wax poetic about race prep, so I really can't talk."

"I run, also. Not as much since I hurt my knee, but I always enjoyed it. Good stress reliever. I mostly do gym work now. I like to box a little sometimes, too."

"I've got the upper body strength of an infant," I joke. "No boxing for me."

"I'll bet that's not true," he says, reaching out and feeling my arm for muscles. He whistles as I flex. "See? Totally ripped. You're not eating pancakes for breakfast, I'd guess."

"Okay, there's a question…to continue our earlier streak. How do you like your pancakes, Grant?"

He cocks his head at me adorably and answers, "Why, Devon, I enjoy them best with butter and drenched in syrup, with a side of bacon, and some black coffee. Perfection." He rubs his stomach, which is so washboard tight, that I know he doesn't eat such things on a regular basis. "You?"

"I'm a chocolate-chip kind of girl," I answer. "Though you're right, I don't eat them often."

"Knew it."

I lift a shoulder and grin at him. "Okay. Your turn."

He ponders this as he takes a bite of fried pickle. "If you could drive any car in the world, what would you drive?"

"Hmm. I'd drive a Ford F150."

"What?" Grant exclaims, his face and tone a mix of doubt and surprise. "No way."

"Yep. Silver. I'd have a big-ass truck, and I'd live on a big ranch out in, like Wyoming or Montana. I'd be like the Pioneer Woman."

Grant chuckles at this, his smile devastating in a way that goes straight to my core. What in the heck is this crazy thing between us?

"We like the same things, I swear," he says. "I do love me a big truck. I like speed, too, so I might also have like a Ducati in the bed of the truck, too, just for those days when I feel like flying."

"Ah, nothing sexier than a Ducati," I agree, nodding furiously. "Okay, my turn. Have you ever broken a limb?"

"A?" he asks with a laugh. "Let's see...I broke my ankle when I was fourteen and decided to try to ski off my parents' roof into a snowbank. I broke three fingers fighting some kid who insulted my girlfriend when I was sixteen. I've broken several ribs and my nose has been broken twice."

My eyes are wide. "That it?"

He shrugs. "Took me a while to find my Zen."

I snort at this. "That's funny. I've never broken any bones, thankfully. I got a couple of concussions playing soccer in middle school but that's about it."

"Yep, had a couple of those in my youth, as well."

"Shocking," I say with a grin.

"Let's see, my turn?" I nod, and he pops a snack into his mouth while he thinks of a question. Finally, he asks, "Would you ever climb Mount Everest?"

Tilting my head to one side, I think about it for a few moments. "Um, maybe? That's not an answer, I suppose. I'm just not sure. On the one hand, I think it would be thrilling in many ways. It would take every ounce of strength you had, not just physically, but mentally and emotionally as well. Spiritually, too, I suppose. And to see the world from that angle? What a trip it must be."

"But?" Grant asks.

"But people die out there. Often. And it's kind of gross. There's tons of trash and the bodies of the dead just left up on that mountain where they will stay, and that's kind of disturbing to me. Plus, it's expensive. I can think of lots of charities that could use that kind of money, if I had it, you know?"

"I can see that," Grant says, nodding. "I guess I can also see the drive behind why people do it, though. Like, pushing yourself and your body beyond the limits of what should be possible. Doing something only a few people will ever do successfully? It feels like it would be such an achievement."

"Agreed," I say. "That's why I'm not sure. I mean, I won't do it. It's not on my bucket list or anything. Talking theoretically though? I'm not sure."

"What is on your bucket list?" Grant asks softly.

"Oh, no, no, sir. My turn. You don't get two questions in a row."

"My bad." Grant grins before muttering, "Rule follower."

I'm a rule follower to the letter, that's true. I have always been uncomfortable with the idea of being in trouble or working outside of established rules or laws. Trouble is just not in my DNA. Gia would say that's reason number five-hundred-seventy-six proving I'm a boring introvert, but oh well, we are what we are.

And the "oh well" speaks for itself when I just shrug in response to Grant's comment before switching the subject and asking, "What's the most embarrassing thing that's ever happened to you?"

He doesn't miss a beat. "It happened when I was a ticket booth operator at an amusement park."

"How hard can it be to sell tickets, dude?" I give him a lopsided, dubious grin.

"Hear me out." He holds up a hand. "I was a teenager when I got this summer job at an amusement park on a big lake. I had hoped to run one of the roller coasters, but I got assigned to this out-of-the-way ticket booth near the marina. It was, like, a five-minute walk to the main part of the park. I worked with this eighty-year-old woman who had been ripping ticket stubs every summer since she was a teenager, and I had this hot, college-student boss. Every day, it was just the three of us and we saw maybe twenty people come through each day. Really boring."

"So far? Still not that bad. Hot boss, old lady, sit on your duff and watch the boats pass by? Wah. Poor baby."

Grant shakes his head. "I'm not to the bad part yet."

"Well, please continue, then."

"So each day, my boss, Kari, would have to go do boss stuff for an hour or two and she'd leave me and Theresa, the old lady, to do our thing. No big deal. But one day, Kari was gone for longer than usual. I was due for a break, and I really needed to use the restroom, but Theresa was on her break for lunch and she was very serious about taking her lunch break on time each day so I'm like, *Oh, I can hold it*, but the more time passed, the more I had to go. I was sixteen, right, and I didn't know what to do, and the closest bathroom is in the boathouse, which would have meant leaving the ticket booth unmanned for however long it took me to run over and get back."

Cringing, I say, "I can see where this is going."

He nods earnestly. "Yeah. So I decide I'm just

going to go. I'll run out into the bushes by the ticket booth and let it rip. But, of course, the minute I whip it out is the minute I hear my boss ask what the hell I'm doing, and I turn around, still peeing, dick in my hand. Well, you can imagine how the rest goes."

I'm cracking up, shoulders shaking as I fill in the end of the story. "Got fired?"

"Yup. I tried to plead my case but to no avail. Totally mortifying."

The thought of this suave, handsome man as a lanky teenager, getting caught literally with his pants down in front of his pretty boss still has me howling. "Agreed. Yikes."

"What about you?" He tilts his head to one side, eyes sparkling with amusement.

"Mine also has to do with a job situation when I was younger. I was working in a bookstore on my college campus. It was buy-back season and people were in and out all day trying to recoup some of the cost of their overpriced textbooks. So this guy comes in and he's a little cute and he's kind of flirty while I'm scanning his books, and when I finish, he says he's got to run out to his car because he forgot one. So I'm like, *Yeah, cool*, and then he leans in and says, *You're fly as hell*."

"He called you *fly*?" Grant asks with a laugh. "What year was this? How old was this guy?"

"It's a terrible line, right? So I tell him thanks, I'm flattered, but I have a boyfriend and he's like, *okay, yeah, I just thought I'd let you know.* But he has this weird look on his face. I chalk it up to rejection and move on to the next customer, but I see him walk over and say something to my coworker, who's shelving books a couple of aisles over, before he goes out to get the book he forgot. A few moments later, my coworker comes over and says, *that guy told me to tell you your fly is down.*"

"Oh, geesh," Grant groans. "That's harsh."

"Yeah," I say, cracking up at the memory. "I look down and I'm in black pants, but my fly is wide open, red underwear showing. Humiliation at def-con ten. I ran to the bathroom and hid out until my coworker came to tell me the guy was gone."

Shoulders shaking with laughter, Grant shakes his head. "That's a good one. Holy moly."

It's nearly three in the morning when I look at the clock, surprised at how fast the time has gone. We've long finished our drunk-snacks, and we've just been talking for hours, sharing stories, laughing. It's like we've known each other for months or years, not hours. And when Grant reluctantly says he should get some shut-eye before an early flight in the morning, a pit in my stomach reminds me that I'll probably never see him again.

Rallying, I nod. "Yeah, I've got an early conference session, too. It's probably best if we say good night." I hope I don't sound too forlorn about it, though I probably do.

Grant goes about the task of finding his random clothing items, now wrinkled from lying in heaps all over the floor. He dresses, still looking like a model even in his rumpled, post-sex state. If anything, I find him even sexier that way, because I know it's because of me. Because of what we experienced together.

And I wish I could experience it again, but I suppose it's just not meant to be.

7

i should've told her

Grant

I lean in and kiss her one more time, just wanting one more moment to cling to from this night. Devon is amazing. She doesn't put on airs. She's funny and smart. She's obviously gorgeous. Fuck, why did I have to find this woman tonight?

"I really enjoyed spending time with you tonight," I say, pulling away from the best lips I've ever kissed. "You're amazing."

She bites down on her bottom lip and a flush spreads across her cheeks at the compliment. "Thanks. I feel the same."

The words kind of catch in my throat, which makes me think I shouldn't let them loose, out into the world, but I'm a sucker, so I do it anyway. "Do you want to maybe exchange numbers? Stay in touch?"

There's a heartbeat of thought before she sort of squares her shoulders, like she's trying to convince herself her answer is really what she wants. I know what she'll say before she says it. "No...I think...I like what we did. I like you. A lot. But let's just leave it here?"

I nod, a sharp action that belies the disappointment I feel. She's right, of course. We had a good night, but what would be the point of staying in touch? I'm just out of a disastrous marriage. I'm moving here. She's from who-knows-where.

"You're amazing," I say for the second time. "Seriously. Enjoy your conference."

My feet feel like lead weights as I walk to the door to let myself out. Aside from being extremely reluctant to leave this beautiful woman, something else nags at me. Something I should've told her hours ago.

I get to my room and head for the shower, trying to calm the strange anxiety that has uncoiled itself in my stomach. Should I go back and leave my number with her? Not just because I want to see her again, but also because, well, I think the condom may have broken a little.

Just a little. Most of it was still there, but some cum definitely leaked out as I pulled it off.

It's probably not a big deal. But I should've told her, right? Just in case?

I think about my years with Margot. About the many times we tried to make a baby. I've always wanted to be a father, and while Margot was always somewhat reluctant, we did try, with no luck. Every month, her cycle came like clockwork, and with each disappointment, I came closer to truly believing that the problem was me. I suggested we go to a fertility specialist just to make sure. Did my swimmers work okay? Margot always told me I was too anxious about it, wanted it too much. She told me many times that she had read stories about couples that got pregnant after simply relaxing about it. She told me it would happen when it was meant to happen, and that she didn't really want to have sex just to make a baby. It made her feel like a machine and took the romance out of the whole experience.

I could see what she meant. I calmed, stopped worrying about it so much. Just in time to find out she had started sleeping with one of my best friends.

When Margot and I met, she was fun and sassy and really into the idea of having this transient life. She liked traveling for games, seeing new places. But over time, I saw how the travel wore on her, how she wanted something more settled. And when I got hurt, when the game ended for me, I thought that it would be a good thing to be around more, to think about settling, finding some permanence. I thought things would be good, better for her, but we just ended up falling apart.

In a way, I blame myself. I was extremely focused on having a family, and she never really was. We weren't on the same page about it, and if she felt like I'd turned her into some kind of baby-making machine? I mean, I tried to show her I loved her all the time, that I wanted to make a little human with her because of that love. I suppose I didn't do a good enough job of it, though. And well, I guess I don't blame her for looking for passion and connection somewhere else. *But* she could have ended our marriage *before* she sought that. I loathe disloyalty. I would never have cheated on her, but if I'd been unhappy, I know I would have ended things. *So, her infidelity still pisses me right the fuck off. And what Graves did too, the shit bag.*

Tonight was an eye-opener for me. Meeting Devon was like a dream. She's gorgeous, funny, and smart. And the sex? It was the best I can recall. Honestly, I forgot sex could be that good.

Just thinking about it makes me hard again. With the warm water sluicing over me, I grip the base of my cock, moving back and forth as I relive every moment with Devon. Her dark hair and eyes, the sound of her moans of pleasure, the feel of her warm pussy, the taste of it, the feel of her mouth around my cock.

It doesn't take long for me to explode again, a sharp huff of a moan letting loose from my lips as I empty myself. God, I haven't felt like this in so, so long. It's like being a teenager with a crush on a pretty girl. Can't wait to see her again. Can't control myself around her.

I sigh as I finish washing my orgasm away, disappointed I won't be seeing this woman ever again.

Still, I should probably go back and tell her about the condom. It's the right thing to do. So, I dry off and throw on a pair of basketball shorts and a new Crush hoodie that I picked up in the team store before I left the arena after my interview. I make my way back to Devon's room, knocking lightly on the door. It's very late, and there is no doubt in my mind that she was very tired when I left, so I'm not surprised when she doesn't answer. I wait longer than necessary, hoping she'll appear, hoping I can see her one more time.

Finally, I trudge back to my room, falling into the bed, my eyes heavy but my mind still buzzing from maybe the craziest day of my entire life.

I'll try to reach Devon again in the morning.

I just need to see her one more time.

8
i had a little adventure

Devon

As I wake, my eyes practically stuck together, I stretch, finding every muscle in my body hurts. It's different from any workout ache I've ever had.

Blinking away the grogginess, I consider sleeping in, staying in my cocoon of fluffy white blankets, and skipping the first session of the morning. However, the rule follower in me wins out, and I force myself to throw my legs over the side and push myself upright. I check the clock and am surprised at the time. Even having stayed up way past my bedtime, I still woke up in time for a morning workout.

I dress for the gym and head down to get in a run on the treadmill, followed by some light weight work. I'm sluggish and slow-moving, but I make it happen and work up a good sweat, feeling less guilty about the junk I ate early this morning. I keep watching the door to the gym, hoping Grant might come in, but I remember he said he had an early flight. He's probably long gone. Which sucks.

Back in the room, I hit the shower. Still moving slowly, I savor the luxurious hot water and the smell of soap and shampoo as I massage at my aching muscles. The spot between my legs is sore, in a *very* good way that only reminds me of the night. Of sexy Grant.

Wow. Wow, wow, wow. I've never had such wild chemistry with someone. My ex and I had fun for a while, but it didn't take long for me to realize that I was really married to his ego. I was arm candy, which does not a solid marriage make.

Shawn has long moved on from me, from our relationship. I'm okay with it, really, but I think the whole experience soured me on the idea of "true love." I thought I had it with my husband, until I didn't. And I've dated, but no one has really kept my attention. I've been out with a few guys since I moved to Las Vegas, but none of them has been remarkable. Nice. Successful. Good-looking men, all of them, but I've felt nothing. Nothing. I've started to wonder if something is wrong with me.

Grant, though? I think he could keep my attention for a good, long while. From the minute I saw him, I wanted him. The sex was *so* hot. Amazing, really. But more than that? We could talk to each other. We had things in common. He was real and honest and funny. I truly enjoyed being in his company.

Maybe I made a mistake in not exchanging numbers with him. Maybe we could have built something real.

A weird, delirious sound escapes. Something real? With a one-night stand? That's just *downright crazy talk*, as my grandma Josephine would say. No one makes a life with a guy they meet at a hotel bar. No one makes something real with someone they took to bed after a few drinks and some nice conversation. I know this. He knows this. And that's why I said we needed to go our separate ways with no strings.

It was the right thing to do.

But what I really need to do is let the thought of Grant be what it is—a perfectly lovely memory. A great time. Our instant connection and rapport still surprises. I can't recall the last time I felt so comfortable with someone other than Gia, if I'm honest. Every time I think about how awed Grant was —*at being with me*—and how freaking hot the sex was —how attentive and lustful *he* was—I blush. To think that Gia had reprimanded me for staying in the hotel to get the feeling of being away from home. *And what a feeling it was.* But...I had a little adventure with a really sexy guy. That was it.

Steeling myself, I decide I'm done thinking about this. It was fun, but it's over. Time to move on. But...

Oh shit. I forgot to text Gia.

Wrapped in my towel, I find my phone and the seventeen texts and calls from Gia, checking in to make sure I'm not the victim of a gorgeous serial killer.

Gia: You ok?

Gia: Seriously.

Gia: Do I need to come back there?

Gia: Guy's not a creeper, right?

Gia: Assuming you're not dead in a ditch somewhere.

Gia: This is not like you, D.

Gia: I sure hope you're getting some.

Gia: Sex is the only reason I will forgive you for making me worry.

Devon: Sorry. All good.

Devon: Really, really good. More later.

Without waiting for a response, I dry off and get ready for the day, pulling on a pair of skinny pants with a tank top and a long cardigan with my favorite pair of peep-toe heels. My long hair is down around my shoulders, and I'm toying with the idea of pulling it back for the day when a knock sounds at the door.

When I open the door wide, I'm shocked to find Grant there. Looking tall, dark, and delicious in a navy-blue pullover simply paired with jeans, he is every bit as classy and gorgeous dressed down as he is in a suit, and I find myself unable to come up with any real words to greet him.

Why am I so tongue-tied by this man?

"Hey," he says, giving me a panty-dropping, lopsided grin.

"Uh. Hey?"

"Can I step inside for a minute?" He looks at his Apple watch. "I've got about ten minutes before I need to head to the airport."

I gesture for him to step inside, which he does. When he turns, he looks sheepish, like he's about to admit something.

I blurt out, "You're married. You came to tell me you're married."

His eyes go wide, but then he chuckles. "No. I was, until fairly recently, but I'm not anymore."

"Oh, well, that's good," I say, giving a weak smile that probably makes me feel like a ridiculous fool.

He looks me up and down, and the weight of it makes me feel all kinds of ways that I'm sure would take more than ten minutes to work out.

"I actually came to tell you something I should have told you last night. I think that condom tore a bit. I can't be sure if it happened as I was taking it off or what, but it was mostly full, so I don't think it's a big deal."

"Not a big deal?" I ask lamely, my voice sounding tinny even to my own ears.

Grant reaches out and puts his hand in mine. He looks me straight in the eyes as he says, "Hey. My ex-wife and I tried for years to get pregnant, and it never happened. I don't think I can...well, you get it. I think it would have happened long ago if my swimmers were swimming."

My stomach twists in an ugly display of anxiety, but I nod. "I'm sure it's fine. I mean, it's probably fine."

Grant is still holding my hand. He says, "I'm sorry I didn't tell you last night. I came back and knocked, but you didn't answer."

I'm not sure what to say, honestly. I'm not mad, not really. I haven't had to navigate this, and since he was married until recently, my guess is he hasn't either. And I believe him when he says he doesn't think he can get anyone pregnant.

"I fell asleep straight away," I say. "Thought about staying in bed this morning, too. I confess that our evening really wore me out."

Another panty-dropping grin. And a dimple I didn't notice last night. Swoon.

"Well, our activities were pretty...active," Grant says. "I loved it all."

He actually blushes, which melts my heart in all new ways. I pull my hand free and grab the hotel notepad and a pen, writing my number on it and ripping it from the pad. I hand it to Grant and say, "If you ever feel like learning my favorite childhood activity or my favorite pizza toppings, give me a call."

Grant takes the piece of paper and folds it, slipping it into his pocket. He leans in, his lips meeting mine, and I feel that now-familiar warmth spread through my abdomen, his effect still strong, in the daylight, without alcohol.

When he pulls away, he looks reluctant. I know the feeling.

"I should go, or I'll miss my flight."

I nod. "I know."

"It was really good to meet you, Devon."

"You, too."

He kisses my forehead. His lips linger there as I close my eyes, inhaling the scent of him, hoping I can hold it in my memory for a long, long time.

Grant backs away, reaches out, touches my face one more time.

And then he leaves.

He just goes out the door and away to wherever he came from.

Did I just say a farewell I'm going to regret?

9

move on, start fresh

Grant

I'm eyeballing a random kitchen appliance, trying to decide whether to move it or donate it, when the front door opens and Margot steps inside.

I must look surprised, because she says, "Used my key," before flashing the item in question.

"Do you want this...whatever it is?" I ask, holding up what I think is a rice cooker. "I made a pile of things I'm not moving. If you want them, please take them."

She looks around the house, now empty of artwork, photos, books, and adornments. Margot always took a lot of pride in how our home was decorated. She took many of her favorite things when we split up, but it still looked nice, still looked like the home we had built together. Now, everything is packed up and it just looks like an empty shell. *Pretty indicative of our marriage...well, what happened to it.*

"This doesn't look like our house anymore," she says, reading my thoughts.

"No, you're right."

"We made so many memories here. It's kind of sad."

"Well, sad things happen when you screw my best friend in my own bed." A bit harsh? Yeah, but whatever. "A bed I sold, by the way. I'll be buying a new one that is free of memories once I get to Vegas."

Margot's lips curl downward, but she doesn't take the bait. Which is good; I'm not in the mood to have it out with her. She wanders over toward the discard pile but stops at the kitchen counter, her fingers grazing a piece of paper there. Shit. That's Devon's number. Not that Margot would know from her name, but the message is a different story. *Call me. Devon. 656-551-3174*

"Pot calling the kettle black much?" she says with a sneer. "Seems like maybe you've already got a bed to warm in sunny Las Vegas?"

"Nope," I answer, eyeing a vegetable spiralizer that I will surely never use. "You slept with someone in my bed while we were married. I slept with someone after we got divorced. Two totally different things. And also none of your business."

"Well, for the record, I think you're totally running

away from things by taking this job. So much easier to just pack it all up and leave."

I look up with a heavy sigh. Margot is a beautiful woman; she always has been and always will be. But now, when I see her standing there with her bleach-blonde hair and bright blue eyes, she just looks like any woman I could pass on the street. Whatever was between us for all those years is long gone. She's like a stranger to me. My mind instantly compares her to Devon. God, what a woman. Not just her body, or her skin, or her hair. God, her hair...Devon was the whole package. Funny. Self-deprecating. Smart. Sexy. I should have called her by now. I'm an idiot.

Margot seems to be waiting for me to answer her ridiculous claim, so I shake thoughts of Devon from my head and say, "So what? What's there to stay for, Margot? I'm not interested in staying in a town where my ex-wife is shacked up with my ex-friend. I don't think there's a person out there who would fault me for that. Plus, this is an amazing career opportunity. Why the hell would I pass up a GM job with a Cup-winning all-star team? It'd be fuckin' stupid to pass it up, regardless of my personal situation."

"That's exactly the point, Grant," Margot fires back. "It's always about *you*. About what *you* want. About *your* career. I had to follow you around while you played, and you would have made me move again for this year, whether I wanted to or not."

I can't help but smart from the verbal lashing, even

though it's not the first time I've heard it. Even though we talked about the reality of my life when we first got together. She knew what she was getting into, and, at first, she mostly liked the excitement of being in the stands and being married to a professional athlete. After eleven years, I'm sure she felt differently, but for a long time, it was just reality, and we faced it head-on together. And then we had those years where I wasn't even playing. Although, she's now fucking another former hockey player.

Why bother with this conversation? We're done. *But...*"Why are you doing this? We're not together anymore. We've already been to this particular rodeo, why get on that horse again?"

"I'm pregnant," she blurts, her hand instinctively moving to her stomach.

What. The. Fuck. What does she mean she's pregnant? "Well, that proves it then," I say, mostly to myself.

"Proves what?"

"My swimmers are defective. All those years of trying...it tore us apart, and now you're..." I let out a weird sound, kind of a huff and a bitter laugh combined.

"Barton's really excited," Margot says, her tone softer now. "He's always wanted kids."

"*I've* always wanted kids." I grit my teeth, shake off the frustration and anger, and say, "You know what, congrats to you both. I mean it. I'm happy for you."

Margot looks away, her eyes swimming with tears suddenly, and I get the distinct impression that while Barton might be happy, his baby mama may not feel quite the same.

"I just...I wasn't expecting it. That's all." But she forces a smile and adds, "Everything happens for a reason, though, right?"

Chewing on my bottom lip, I don't have an answer for her, so I go back to cleaning out the kitchen cupboards. "If there's anything you want, just take it. And put the key on the counter when you leave."

Still being harsh, but it's all I can manage without being outright hostile. Without raging, which is what I'm doing on the inside. *Years of trying for a family.* There is so much bitterness burning inside me.

Margot stares at me for a solid minute or two before she finally realizes I'm done. I'm not saying another word. I can't. She puts the key on the counter and leaves, the door clicking quietly behind her.

It's not until several heartbeats after that click I let myself breathe again. I sit on the floor of the kitchen and force myself to get air, trying to clear my mind.

She's pregnant. She's pregnant. She's pregnant.

It just repeats over and over and over again.

She's fucking pregnant.

I wanted a family with her. *I* wanted that with her. I'm staring down the front side of forty, and I always imagined I'd be a dad by now. We tried for eight years. Eight fucking years, and it just...Did. Not. Happen. It took four years of begging to even get her to start trying with me. And once she finally agreed? It was month after month of disappointment. Every time her period came, it felt like a gut punch. Every year that went by, I felt like a failure. I mean, it's not like we got pregnant, and she lost it. It simply never happened at all.

When I suggested IVF or adoption, she was an immediate hard no. She said she couldn't take it anymore. We'd been fighting a lot. She said things had gotten forced, mechanical, and she wasn't wrong. She tried to get me to relax about it, but I couldn't, and it ruined us. I've owned the blame for that, as I should.

Two months after the IVF conversation, I came home early one afternoon and found her in bed with Barton. My friend and colleague of two decades. They had it going on for a while, I guess, but I never saw it.

I suppose that's telling of how the situation was with us. But no one deserves infidelity. No one. And even though I'm over it—and certainly don't feel the sting of pain I once felt—it was devastating being betrayed by two people I loved and cared deeply about. *Who obviously didn't feel the same way about me and our marriage.*

I'm not the kind of guy who can't admit to his own shortcomings. It's easy to make Margot the bad guy in all of this, and for the infidelity, she is. But I can acknowledge how much I let her down as a husband —as her best friend—so there's that. The relationship was undeniably over long before it ended. She had clearly left our marriage emotionally way before she left it physically. She made choices to ensure that. There are no residual feelings for Margot.

So, it's time. Time to move on.

Time to start fresh.

I get to my feet and take a deep breath, surveying the rest of the work I need to do to get ready for the movers. Devon's note sits lonely on the counter. A beacon maybe? Is this why I've held on to it these last couple weeks closing out my life up here in Alberta? I do think about calling her. I've *thought about it* every single day since I returned from my interview. But what would I say? I don't know anything about her. Where she lives. What she does for a living. Her last name. What would be the point?

Vegas is a fresh start, and I need my head in the game in this new gig. I chalk Devon up as a really great memory, toss her number in the trash, and decide to focus only on the future from here on out.

10
fit 2 cook

Devon

The teaching kitchen I've rented is small, but it should work fine for today's class. My long-term goal is to hard launch Fit 2 Cook LLC next year with several long-term nutrition clients, fully fleshed-out cooking classes, with the release of an accompanying cookbook. I've got a whole business and PR plan, so right now, I'm just testing things out and building some word-of-mouth.

It's not that I don't love my job with the Crush. I do very much. It's been challenging and rewarding in ways I never thought possible. But after seeing Holly start her own business (she gave me lots of PR advice for my own ideas), I felt like it might be the right time to branch out and do my own thing.

So, this is night one of the test kitchen. I want to do group cooking classes that are based on participants' individual nutrition needs. It's fun to do a class together, the energy is always great, but usually, everyone has to cook the same thing and sometimes they don't want or like that. It ends up being a missed opportunity. So I've got options for each class. If you need more lean protein in your diet, there's an option for that. If you want to go vegan, there's an option for that. It's all personally tailored—a fresh niche. In my market research, I couldn't find anyone else in the area offering anything comparable right now.

And Vegas is ripe with potential clientele. There are a bazillion athletes and performers who have very specific nutritional needs. Caloric intake, high protein, weight management. These people have grueling training and performance schedules, and it can be really hard for them to manage their nutrition. Like, can I just say how many hockey players I find shoving burgers and fries in their faces in the arena pub every day after practice?

The book I'm writing is tailored to my ideal clientele. I've already got a publisher; now I just need to finish writing. I'm hoping these sessions will give me a sense of what kinds of questions it should answer.

Gia is the first to arrive, always my cheering squad. She says, "Let's cook the shit out of this bitch," as she walks in, which makes me cringe-laugh.

A few minutes later, the rest of my test class comes in. Two of my hockey players—starting winger

Mikhail and rookie winger Aiden—come in and plop down on stools at the back of the class.

"What is this, church?" I ask with what I hope does not sound like a nervous laugh. I hope it sounds like a confident, fun laugh, rather than the laugh of a woman who's so anxious that her feet are sweating. I know, so gross, right?

The guys laugh, and Mikhail says, "We're big. Don't want to impede anyone's view."

I roll my eyes but then understand as three young women come in and take seats in the row in front of them. They're all backup dancers for a big A-list singer's Vegas show, and they are teeny-tiny little things. Gia does bookings for the hotel where they perform, so I have her to thank for luring them to my class.

"Hey, everyone," I say once they're all in place. "I'm Devon Pearson. Right now, I'm the full-time nutritionist for the Vegas Crush."

My two hockey dudes *woot-woot* in the back, fists pumping in the air. I pump my fist back at them with a grin. "I also have a side gig called Fit 2 Cook, which I hope to launch into a full-fledged business next year. You are my guinea pigs, so thanks in advance for letting me try some things out on you. Any feedback, thoughts, or ideas, I want to hear them. This is about creating the best experience possible for my clients, so I need the good, the bad, and the ugly or I won't be able to achieve that. Cool?"

I earn a bunch of nods and thumbs-up in response.

"Okay, so this class is designed to be as personalized as possible. I want to help you design a meal plan tailored to your specific needs, and also easy to prepare. I know you don't have much time..."

"Or talent in the kitchen," Mikhail says, making everyone laugh.

"Speak for yourself," Aiden says, grinning and winking at the dancers. "I'm magic in the kitchen."

I'm thankful for the banter because it helps me feel less nervous. "Well, whatever your skill levels, I still know how much time you give to your jobs and how much your jobs require of your body. So I want to help you make sense of what your body needs and wants when it comes to fuel."

I have everyone take a minute to write out an average weekly menu. "Whatever you normally eat. I promise, there will be no judgment. I just want to understand what your baseline is. There may be reasons you're craving fried foods or sugary treats. I want to help you make sense of it and then find the best choices to fill those needs."

While most of the class follow directions, Gia and Mikhail spend the bulk of their time flirting with each other. Their banter is actually pretty funny, but I still elbow Gia as I pass, stopping in front of Aiden's workstation.

"Welcome to the Crush," I say. "We haven't met officially."

"Aiden Kennedy," he says, holding out a hand to shake.

"Nice to meet you officially. I read your stats and bio when they brought you onto the roster. You played at Yale?"

He nods. "Dumbest smart guy in Connecticut."

"Oh, I'm sure that's not true, Aiden, but I'm not sure we've ever had an Ivy League player at the Crush, so at least there's that claim to fame."

Aiden, a tall, lean muscled man, definitely has some of the iconic Kennedy charm goin' on, with his dark locks with just a hint of curl and a dimple in one cheek. He probably makes the ladies swoon like nobody's business. I mean, the majority of those guys do, to be honest. I'm mostly oblivious, but I know the single ones are all out doing the bunny hop much of the time. *Sexuality and the Professional Athlete*. There's a book title for ya. I'd have plenty of source material from the players I've worked with during my time with the Crush.

I head to the front and ask folks to read off their weekly menus, starting with Mikhail, who was clearly not doing the assignment. Serves him right to go first.

"I am a basic kind of guy," he says, looking down at his paper as if there's actually something written on it. He smiles kind of sheepishly as he continues. "I eat two bowls of cereal for breakfast usually. One or two days a week, I stop for scrambled eggs, bacon, and toast on my way to work. I don't usually eat lunch, but

I eat a hamburger at the pub every day after practice. Sometimes I order a pizza later at night, too."

My stomach literally turns at the word "hamburger," and also at the thought of having one every day of the week. I'm not anti-hamburger, but geesh. Moderation. I fight back the urge to throw up just thinking about all the meat grease.

"That is...not an optimal diet. Not gonna lie," I manage to say, holding my hand to my stomach.

"Hey, you said no judgment," he protests.

"I did, I did, you're right," I answer, holding up my hands. "I'm sorry. Just getting a baseline. But, for the record, your baseline is going to lead you to a heart attack if you stick to that list. Just putting that out there."

He narrows his eyes at me in response, but he's smirking, so I know he realizes I'm joking. Kind of. He says, "Don't tell Coach."

This gets a laugh out of me. "What happens at Fit 2 Cook stays at Fit 2 Cook. Besides, I'm going to beat the hamburgers right out of your diet, and you're going to feel and play like a champion, and then there won't be anything to tell Coach other than how healthy you are."

"I'm already a champion," Mikhail says with kind of a sexy tone that I realize is directed to Gia, who's blushing a lovely shade of hot pink.

"Oh boy," I say with a sigh. "Okay, Aiden, you're up."

After going through everyone's weekly menus, I ask them to think about just one thing they could adjust for the next week, and I ask them to write down their long-term fitness and nutrition goals so I can prep for next week's class. We finish by cooking a meal as a group. When it's all finished, we have a nice beet salad with marinated chicken and goat cheese. A homemade vinaigrette tops it, and even the naysayers about beets end up admitting it tastes delicious.

After cleaning up, I tell everyone how excited I am to work with all of them. "We'll cook together and learn from each other. See you next week!"

I'm grabbing my purse as I call over to Gia if she wants to run when we get back to our apartment complex. All I hear in response is, "Um," and it's a humming, question-mark kind of sound. I turn, confused, because we run almost every night, but then I see Mikhail lingering at the door, his heavily tatted arms crossed across his chiseled, tight T-shirt-wearing chest. That boy looks like Trouble. Capital *T*.

"Okay, okay," I say, waving her off. "Don't do anything I wouldn't do."

Gia just winks before taking Mikhail's arm and heading out into the night.

As I lock up, my mind makes its way to Grant. *Again.* If you put Mikhail and Grant side by side, they'd be similar in a lot of ways, minus the tattoos. Both men are handsome. *Quick-witted. Sexy.*

I'm not naive. That's not the only reason I'm

thinking of Grant, though. And as has happened many times over the last few weeks, I've wondered if he's been tempted to call me. After he admitted that the condom may have broken, I thought I might hear from him. I never took a morning after pill or anything. If my worst nightmare comes true and I'm pregnant, wouldn't he want to know? *It was a random hookup at a random hotel in Las Vegas, Devon. You shouldn't try to make it more than that.*

But...he was the most attractive man I've ever seen, bar none. And it was the hottest, steamiest, orgasm-iest sex I've ever had, like ever. Our connection wasn't only sexual, and that's also why I've hoped he'd call. He was funny and smart and interesting. And we had things in common.

But whatever. He said he was from Alberta, which is about sixteen hundred miles north of Las Vegas. It would be totally stupid to try to have something with someone so far away. Long-distance things never work out anyway.

By the time I get home, I know I should run, but it's the vibrator in my nightstand and the sustainable imagery of my night with Grant that get my full attention.

11
speaking of magic

Grant

"Giroux and Cross?" I ask before taking a bite of my bacon. "They did okay in the last Cup final?"

Max Terry sits across from me, digging into an egg white omelet that makes my waffle and bacon look decidedly unhealthy. He nods as he chews. "They did all right. They're not well-integrated into the team, though, from what I can tell. Both men keep to themselves. Cross is a Nervous-Nelly. Giroux's just a bit of a snob."

"And the new rookie?"

"Aiden Kennedy. Winger like Giroux. Did four years at Yale. Trying out some younger guys in case we lose Kaz."

"Is the retirement talk real?" I ask.

He lifts a shoulder. "He hasn't said anything to me and we talk regularly, but he's at a place in his personal life where, if I were him, I'd be thinking about moving into management or coaching."

"Kazmeirowicz is still so good, though."

"He is. And he's a great leader. And he's just really come into his stride the past couple of seasons, honestly. His contract will have him with us another season at least, and then he'll either come looking for more money or he'll retire. We'll deal with it, whichever way it plays out."

"Any trades on the horizon I need to think about?"

"At the moment, no. But that's where I need you. Financially, we're in good shape because we're packing seats. But we've got some seriously hefty contracts with Kazmeirowicz, Kolochev, Demoskev, and Drăghici—or the Ice Dragon as he's affectionately known around here. Lockhardt's contract is nothing to sneeze at, either, and I think Zelenka's agent must be asleep at the wheel, because I'd be demanding more money for him if I was worth my salt in that role."

"He plays a lot of minutes."

"Since he got here. He's been starting for us since his rookie year, which was what, maybe five seasons ago? I don't know where we are with his contract, but I'd bet an extension will cost us a pretty penny."

"And your new goalie?"

"Calum Lefleur," he says, grinning. "Our own personal Sheldon Cooper."

I smirk and raise an eyebrow. "He's a physicist?"

"He's like a savant. Probably could be a physicist.

In fact, I think I heard one of the guys say he could've gone to MIT, but he chose hockey instead. Now that he's engaged to Billie Hirsch, no telling what he'll be doing a few years from now. When your fiancée's career explodes into the stratosphere as hers just did, then maybe we see him playing guitar in her band at some point, you know?"

"Goalies are a strange breed, for sure." The headline story: NHL CHAMPION GOALKEEPER, CALUM LEFLEUR, TO MARRY BILLIE HIRSCH IN CELEBRITY WEDDING OF THE YEAR had been huge mainstream news at the end of last year. There wasn't anybody alive in the sport of hockey or the music industry who didn't know about the goalie who was traded to Vegas from Montreal, met a drummer in a Las Vegas club band and fell in love, and how she wrote her Billboard number one single, "The Keeper," just for him. His Malibu beachside marriage proposal had been captured on video and covered literally by every club's media team in the entire NHL.

"Let's just say, I won't be all that surprised if he hangs up his goalie helmet when his contract's up in another three years, regardless of how many awards and Cups he's earned, or what we could pay him," Max says with a shake of his head.

"If I was married to Billie Hirsch? *I* might even leave hockey and go with her, so I can see his point. Who's to say what any of us would do if we were married to a Grammy-nominated, rock-chick, superstar songwriter/drummer, you know? We all do weird things for love...and also for this tremendous sport."

"Surely do," Max says. "Including spending the bulk of my budget on a first-string."

I chuckle at this. "It's a strategy."

"A strategy that has worked so far. They just have to stay healthy and committed. Evan's injury allowed us to try out Giroux for more minutes and he's solid. He's not a superstar, but he's solid. But beyond that, I think the depth just isn't quite there, which makes me nervous."

"Well, I get the choices you've made. You've invested in the right talent, and it's paid off for you. I also understand why you're worried. You've got big contracts to pay out and a city that expects you to keep giving the championship seasons."

"It's not implausible that we could become a legacy team," Max says. "Look at Golden State. Look at the Patriots. With the right coaching and management, and a constant eye on recruiting and retaining top talent, there's no reason we can't be that for hockey."

"Agreed. I'll take a look, let you know where I think there are opportunities."

"At the end of the day, I want a butt in every seat and an arena so loud it hurts your ears. In order to have that consistently, we can't plateau. We can't backslide."

"Got it. Hearing you loud and clear. You think coaching is strong?"

"Brown is good. Great, really. Underrated, in my opinion."

"The others?"

"They take his lead. I think we're okay on coaching."

"Well, if you're underwhelmed by the talent on the bench, then I think coaching might need to step up its game. They need to pay as much attention to keeping second- and third-string strong and sharp as they do the front line."

"Fair point. Watch a practice or two and let me know your thoughts," Max suggests.

"Sounds good."

We finish eating, and Max takes the bill before offering me a tour of the arena and offices. I've got a whole team of people behind the scenes that I need to get to know now, so we take our time, starting in the administrative offices. I meet the accounting and finance team, the arena operations team, the sales team, and the PR team. A redheaded woman named Scarlett warns me not to drink the water here, and I laugh but then cast a confused glance at Max.

Max sighs. "Cupid has been busy around here the past few seasons. Kazmeirowicz met and married his wife here. Then Kolochev and Demoskev fell like dominoes right behind him. All in spite of a non-fraternization policy, too. Went straight out the window."

"But I'd say it's all for the best, right, Max? The guys are all better because they found us." Scarlett gives Max a cheeky smile and a wink. To me, she says, "Maybe you'll find your soulmate here, too."

"Oh, already had a wife. I don't need another one for now."

"Making a note of that," Scarlett says, tapping a finger to her temple. "We'll make sure to get you on Vegas' hottest bachelors list."

"*Anyway,*" Max emphasizes, changing the subject away from the love lives of the players and staff, "I'm sure Scarlett and her team will have you up here getting your photo taken and blasting out your personal information on social media in no time."

We head out of the office to tour the rest of the facility, finishing on the lower level with the locker rooms, weight room, and physical therapy offices. I meet Georg Kolochev's wife, Pam. I remember seeing the replays of her over-the-top marriage proposal to him in a Playboy Bunny suit, and she's just as cheeky as I might have expected. I like her, though, even more as she walks me through the philosophy of the physical therapy team.

Max tells me how she and her husband, Georg Kolochev, are in the process of adopting defensive teammate Tyler Lockhardt's very young brother and sister after a custody emergency in the family.

"This place is kind of one big loving family, isn't it?" I say more to myself than to Max as we walk down the hall.

"It is," Max answers. "I think that's one of the reasons the team has such magic on the ice. It would be hard to replace."

"I confess, the more I learn, the more I realize how unique this team is." It certainly wasn't like this in Alberta. This level of team loyalty is matchless. *But vital for success.*

"Look, I'm not throwing Bud under the bus—because he really got us to where we are now—but he was a little clueless about this stuff. He didn't think about the chemistry of the whole organization. He didn't realize what kind of magic was happening. I'm glad you see it already. It further proves you're the right guy for the job."

"Well, I appreciate the confidence you've placed in me."

We stop in front of a half-open door to what looks to be little more than a closet. Max says, "Speaking of magic. This is our nutritionist's office. She's been great with the guys. Got Kolochev off the sauce. I think you'll be impressed with her work with the team. Just hoping she's in so you can meet her today."

He pushes the door open, and I swear I just about swallow my own tongue.

"Devon Pearson," Max says, "Meet our new GM, Grant Gerard."

Devon's brown eyes go wide with surprise, but she recovers quickly, standing and brushing off the front of her skirt, holding out a hand for me to shake.

I take her hand and clear my throat. "Nice to meet you." It comes out more like a question. I keep shaking her hand for longer than I need to because her skin is just as soft as I remember. *And she's really fucking beautiful...just as I remember. Wait. Devon works* here?

Aw, fuck!

Yeah, that.

That precise thing.

I've fucked one of my employees.

Well, technically, not my direct report, but a few rungs down. Not that it makes it any less awkward.

Fuuuck.

Figures that the one night I let myself go, throw caution to the wind, and it was with a woman I can't have. *I can't be with an employee.*

What are the chances?

But hold up here for just a goddamn minute.

I can't let one slightly tipsy night mess with my dream job.

It was a one-time thing with Devon, and we were both okay with it. When I asked her if she wanted to keep in touch, she told me no. She said she wanted to leave our night together as a great time and keep it there in the past. And I agreed.

As I back away, I realize Max has asked Devon a

whole question to which she is answering, and I haven't heard a thing she's said about the team's nutrition program. As I tune back in, Devon is talking about working with the guys on customizable nutrition plans. She laughs as she says that the arena pub is going to want to put a hit out on her, because she's about to do a dent in their lunchtime hamburger business.

I laugh but it comes out sounding fake, at least to me it does, and I frown to myself, only to find Devon's smile falter as a result.

Awkward much?

"Well, it was nice to meet you, Devon. Thanks for what you do," I say, stepping toward the door. I know I'm being cold. I don't want to be, but fuck. Flashes of our night together invade my brain, her off-the-chain sexy cries when she was coming underneath me...how she stared up at me when *I* was coming *in* her.

I blow out a breath and step into the hallway, hoping my dick will stay firmly under my immediate control. No need to sport a hard-on in front of the team's owner and a new employee.

Holy hell. I need to get it together.

Focus, Gerard—on facts.

Devon's an incredibly beautiful, funny, smart, and lovely woman who's amazing in bed, but still...just someone I hardly know. We can get through this. We'll laugh it off later. *I hope.*

It's not until I get onto the elevator, trying hard to

focus on whatever Max is saying about some capital repairs needed on this level, that I let out a breath I didn't even know I was holding.

Devon is here in Vegas.

And we'll be working in the same building.

So much for *throwing away* the past and starting fresh in Las Vegas.

12
the new gm of the crush

Devon

*T*hat did not just happen.

But it just did!

The extremely hot guy I had sex with a few weeks ago was not just in my office.

But he just was.

Oh my God. This is not possible. He can't be the new GM. I sit back down in my office chair, totally shell-shocked. I mean, I knew Bud had retired at the end of the season and they had been interviewing for the role around that time. And they sent out an email a week ago saying they were bringing on board someone named Grantham Gerard. Frankly, I didn't pay much attention and it didn't have a picture attached.

Oh, Christ on a ham sandwich. This is a whole hot mess.

Despite the duds I've dated over the years, and the

fact that I'm divorced, I still have hope that true love and soulmates exist. I may have joked around here and there that I'd like to find my own hockey hunk to enjoy, but I wasn't at all serious in regards to players *who play for the Vegas Crush.* Pam's bachelorette party comes to mind when Scarlett told us how she slept with Viktor in a moment of sexual weakness. It sounded romantic and all, but for one irrevocable rule. I never, ever, ever date my coworkers.

Plenty have asked or flirted, and others may have flouted the non-fraternization policy, but not me. No way. I'm not at all interested in crossing that line. I am a rule follower to the nth degree.

I am genuinely happy for the people who have fallen in love around here. Truly. But I'm only interested in keeping things totally professional here at work. I just want to do my job and go home. No added worry or stress, which dating a colleague would certainly create for my anxious self. No. Nope. Dating a colleague is not on my to-do list.

Not that I'm dating Grant Gerard.

The new General Manager of the Vegas Crush Organization.

Who is gorgeous, nice, *and* a total rock star in bed.

Oh Christ.

Nope. Nope. I will not flip out here. We were two consenting adults. He wasn't the GM yet when it happened. We had a fun night, and we agreed that was all. I gave him my number on a whim, and he didn't call, and I'm okay with that. Honestly, I'm glad for it. It made things easier. Cleaner. And especially now. *Thank God his fear about the condom breaking didn't end up being an issue.* I think that's the second time I've thought that, too, but it's even more imperative now. *Which means, we both have to keep things professional.* No lusting after the sexy new GM.

His demeanor was so weird today, anyway. He was short and closed off and clearly uncomfortable. Which I get. I sure as hell wasn't expecting to see him, so why would he be expecting to see me?

And he needs to distance himself. He's the GM. *FFS—For. Fuck's. Sake.* He cannot cross boundaries like that. Grant is the new guy with lots to prove and this is probably a very big deal for his career. No messing around with the staff. That would be a bad look right off the bat. Well, it would always be a bad look. Players and staff are one thing. I've never seen anyone from management go down the fraternizing path.

It takes several steadying breaths for me to get my pulse back to normal, to clear the panic and anxiety. I pull up a search engine and plug in Grant's name. I don't know why I didn't in the first place, when the email first went out.

Pictures from all throughout his career pop up. Good lord, he's gorgeous. Heat and want pools between my legs, and I squirm uncomfortably. *I have seen all of that man.* Every glorious inch. Of *every* part. In living color.

Flushed, I turn my attention to the bio I should have read in the company email about his hiring. Thirty-nine years old, he's one of those men who only gets better looking with age. Still, he's eleven years older than me, not that it matters because we won't be anything but colleagues from here on out.

Reading more, I find out he played center for three NHL teams, played for the Cup twice, winning once, and played for the gold medal-winning Canadian team in the Olympics. A year later, he had a career-ending injury and went to the AHL as a middle-manager. A good one, I take it, from the comments calling him a "rising star in sports management." I'm sure he's good at what he does, but I can only imagine how hard that transition to AHL management must have been for him. A guy like that? With a player pedigree like that? It's probably a little like being taken out of the Wall Street high-rise with a view of the city and being sent to the smallest, darkest, dreary office to peddle penny stocks in the pre-Internet era.

So, yes, the Crush GM position is a good one, a real opportunity to use his experience on and off the ice for the hottest team in the game. I can't get in his way.

I don't notice Pam until she's right behind me, her voice nearly rocketing me out of my chair.

"Watching porn in here?" she asks with a laugh. I try, futilely, to close out my browser windows, but Pam sees the multiple pictures I have of Grant Gerard and gives a long, low whistle. "You were stalking our hot, new GM, I see. Carry on then."

"No, I wasn't stalking." I feel the heat in my cheeks giving away my lie.

"Girl," she says, hands on her hips. "He's a Clark Kent for sure. I'd be stalking him, too, if I was single."

"I wasn't…" I can't even finish the sentence. "He was just in here to meet me, and I was embarrassed because I barely skimmed the email about him when he got hired. I was reading his bio."

"*Reading his bio*," Pam emphasizes, making air quotes. "And looking at PR photos from his Olympic glory days."

She cackles and steps back around my desk.

"Was there a business purpose for your visit, Pamela?" I ask with a forced smile; I *know* she knows I'm giving her only because it's past time for her to stop harassing me with this.

"No," she says with her usual snark. "I actually came to chat about the hot, new GM, but it seems you have already become acquainted."

"Only for like two seconds. He was stand-offish."

"No, he was not," Pam says, pursing her lips. "He was charming and smart and awesome."

"Not to me. He said hello, tuned out when I was talking, and then shot out of here like he was worried he might have gotten cooties."

I don't mention that it was totally because of his

panic over seeing a woman he'd had a one-night stand with a few weeks ago standing in front of him in his new place of employment.

"You sure we met the same guy?" Pam asks.

I raise a shoulder.

"Well, hmm."

I go back to my computer. My actual work, and studiously ignore her. Pam is too observant for my liking, especially now, when I'm wet between the legs and totally ready to go home and work off some of this discomfort with my vibrator in the privacy of my own home.

She sits for long enough to make me further uncomfortable. When I look up, asking, "What?" She just laughs some more.

As she walks out, she says, "Don't drink the water, Pearson. You might be next."

I hear her laughter all the way down the hall.

As hard as I try, I simply cannot get my head into my work after all of this craziness. It's almost lunchtime, so I grab my phone and weave my way through the catacombs and out into the daylight. I call Gia, needing someone to talk to about this crazy twist in my life plot.

"You never call me during the workday," is how my friend answers her phone. "Are you at the hospital or something?"

"No. I can't call my best friend over my lunch break?"

"You're you, so no. What's up?"

"Um, remember that guy? From the hotel?"

"Hot-sex guy? All-night-long guy?"

"Yep, that's the one."

"He called you finally? Or he's married or something and his wife came to wreck you with a hatchet?"

"What? No. No wife. No hatchet."

"But?"

"But he's the new general manager for the Crush."

The line is silent for a few seconds. Then, "Oh, shit."

"Yeah. That's about the same reaction I had when he showed up in my office with the team's owner this morning."

"Did he recognize you?"

"Yeah. He acted super weird. Shook my hand for a beat too long. Tuned out in a way that made me think he was calculating his escape route."

"Probably wasn't expecting his tasty midnight snack to be back on the plate for breakfast."

"It's not—I'm not his midnight snack, you fool."

Gia laughs. "Come on, you know you'd hit that again."

"Sure, if he wasn't like the boss of all of us. I would never sleep with a coworker. Never."

"Well, guess what? You already did."

A weird, strangled groan escapes my throat. "Gia, that is not me. I am not that person. I'm not even the person who does one-night stands with handsome strangers I meet in hotel bars. He was my first."

"Yes, I am aware that you're a big fuddy-duddy and that this was out of your precious comfort zone."

"Don't be a jerk."

Gia laughs. "I'm always a jerk. You love me anyway."

"What do I do?"

"You do your job, mind your business. How often did you interact with the old GM?"

"Hardly at all."

"Well, there you go, then. You'll probably never see him. Top management doesn't slum it in the basement at any business, right?"

"I guess..." I'm not so sure about that. In fact, I think Grant will be a vastly different manager than Bud ever was. Bud, though competent at the job, sort of bumbled around, seeming a bit out of his element on the admin side of things and a little lost in his interactions with personnel. Bud Bellikowski was old-school hockey—a guy who climbed up through the player trenches. No Boston University degree for him. Grant Gerard, on the other hand, is the polar opposite of bumbling. Nor does he come off as a hesitant administrator. He's young and energetic. Sharp and focused in all the ways that Bud could never be, and I'm thinking he'll pay far more attention than his predecessor *ever* did.

"You'll be fine. You didn't know who he was when

it happened and if I know you, you won't let it happen again now that you do know who he is. You're disciplined that way."

"Yeah," I say, taking a deep breath, trying to convince myself of her logic. "You're right. This is in my control. And he's a professional, too. This is a big deal for him and he's not going to cross a line. It will be fine."

As we hang up, I head back to my office, hoping against hope that my—*it will be fine*—turns out to be true.

13
all polished diamonds

Grant

"Let's talk about your starters, just to get it out of the way," I say to Coach Brown and the other six members of the coaching team.

"Strong line, but you know that already," Coach says with a shrug. "Four, five years ago I would have said something like *we've got a lot of raw talent, waiting to be shaped*, but today? All polished diamonds."

"Mikhail Zelenka?" I begin going down my list, needing his feedback on each individual guy, each individual contract.

"Strong from the start. He was a rookie with a chip on his shoulder, but that's mostly because of who his father is. It's tough living up to the legacy of *The Great Zelenka*. But still, he got shit done out there and earned his spot. I don't start rookies often, but he's been good from the get-go. His contract is up in another year. I'm surprised his agent hasn't been knocking on the doors trying to tee up a bigger payday." *Same as Max's take on the situation. I agree with Coach on being judged against a legend like his dad every time he steps onto the ice. That's gotta suck.*

"Boris Drăghici?"

"The Ice Dragon is well worth his ridiculous paycheck. He was a good addition. He's quiet, thoughtful, doesn't cause drama, and a goddamn beast on the ice. No issues with him. He's super fit and strong as an ox. I think he basically works out, plays hockey, plays video games, and spends time with his girlfriend. He's not a partier, doesn't drink. Easy guy to have on the team."

"Okay, that's awesome. Does the team have many partiers anymore? I got the impression a lot of them were settling down."

"I don't pay a lot of attention to it unless it gets in the way of their play, but I do think that's settled a bit —particularly for the front line."

"Good to hear. Evan Kazmeirowicz?"

"He's gone from a B-plus to an all-star A. He was talented and well paid before, but somehow really kicked it into gear in the past few years. He's a real leader. He cares about the players. A great captain."

"Retirement talk? I keep hearing he's ready to head to management because he's got three kids and such."

"Bah," Coach says, waving a hand to dismiss the

thought. "He's in the prime of his game. No way. Just rumors. Don't believe everything you hear."

"Okay, good to know. Tyler Lockhardt?"

"Oh, that kid." Coach throws his head back, sighing in mock exasperation.

I just raise an eyebrow.

"He's good."

"Real good," says Nico, the defensive coach. "Total fire starter."

"Because he's a damn hothead," Coach Brown snaps. "Fans love 'im, though. They love that freaking kid. And you know, he's a bit less crazy since that whole nonsense back in Boston with his mom and his siblings."

"I heard about that. Georg and Pam are adopting the kids?"

"Yeah, it's a really good outcome. Lockhardt got blindsided, I think, with the way things went down in Boston, but he grew up real quick. Totally changed him, that experience."

"And Georg Kolochev? He's still in the game?"

Coach nods. "He's totally cruising. Worked hard to get sober and fit. He was always at Evan's back, but his play is so much better now. They're a one-two punch. I'm happy with his game right now. I give the nutritionist downstairs a big gold star on that one. She's the one who got him on the road to rehab."

This perks my ears. Devon, he means.

I shake myself back to reality before getting lost in

thoughts of her in front of these guys. The coaching staff's time is worth a lot. I need to focus, but it is interesting to know how involved she is in the players' well-being.

Back to the subject at hand. "Viktor Demoskev?"

"Solid as a rock. If anyone retires, I'd guess it would be him, but only because he's a closet softie for his wife and kid. Another baby on the way, too, so things could change for him."

"Really? You think he'd retire?"

"Couple of years, sure. He has a contract to finish, but we've talked about it. He likes coaching and he doesn't want to go out on an injury."

"Who could injure that tank of a dude?" Nico asks.

"True," Coach says with a shrug. "But weirder things have happened."

"Hmm. Interesting. Let's talk about goal tending. Calum Lefleur?"

"Cal's play is strong," Coach says. "Darin?"

Darin, the goalie coach, sits forward. "He's a strange kid, but damn, he's a strong stopper."

"Strange, how?" I ask. "Oh, I think Max called him Sheldon Cooper or something."

The coaches all laugh at this. "He's a unique guy for sure," says Darin. "He comes from a family of scientist professors and he's a bit awkward and a bit arrogant, but he can see the trajectory of a shot like nobody's business. His hockey sense is like no other goalie I've ever worked with. I like him and I like his play."

Coach Brown adds, "He's much more manageable now that he's stopped the broken record about how much he does not want to be here."

"He doesn't want to be here?" Who the hell wouldn't want to be here? This team is on fire right now.

"He didn't want the trade, and he fought it tooth and nail at first. Took him a hot minute to get connected to the team. He's happy and settled now, though. And he's good, so I'm not complaining. He's Darin's responsibility, not mine," Coach says, grinning slightly.

"Do you have a good second-string goalie?" I ask.

"We have a mediocre second-string goalie," Darin answers. "Dante Castellano asked for a trade, and we granted it. He got better, mostly because he was pissed that we pulled Cal over instead of moving him up to starter, but then he took his newfound skills elsewhere. So now we have Beau Couture up from our AHL affiliate, who is decent but needs some refinement and some NHL starts to get into fighting shape."

"How about the others? Giroux? Cross? Kennedy?"

The coaches all squirm for a minute, giving each other the side-eye.

"Giroux and Cross got time in the finals, yeah?" I prod.

"They did. And they did okay. They just don't seem to fit," says Brittani Matthews, who coaches second-string along with O'Dell Williams.

O'Dell nods. "The top guys all have this crazy chemistry. It's palpable when you watch it live. They're not perfect but they are connected. And we're just missing that in the second- and third-string lines. There's not a deep bench."

Coach Brown shoots him a look, and O'Dell raises a shoulder in response. "What? I'm just being honest." *And that's the way I like it. And it will only make the team stronger.*

I watch the body language and then say, "Look, I'm not a coach. I'm not a recruiter. And I'm not here to do those jobs. I just need to know what we need to hold on to and what I can cut loose so we can manage the budget. We have some big-ass contracts and if we're taking on junior-high players for a varsity squad just to fit the budget, then I need to know that so we can fix it. You know what I mean? You are all aware that a deep bench is a necessity for a true shot at a playoff run. Always. And what's the recruiting team doing to scout out the next generation for us? Are we being aggressive about stalking other rosters? And if we leave things as they are, what are we doing to get these guys ready for their big moments?"

The coaches are silent, most looking down at their laps. I don't know if it's because I'm the new guy and they don't trust me or if it's because they don't like this degree of feedback. *Didn't Bud Bellikowski ask these kinds of questions?*

"Well, I thank you all for your input and your work," I say, standing. "This is a top-notch team and I'm excited to be here. If there's anything you want or need to talk about, my door is always open."

The coaching staff all stand, murmuring their thanks before heading out. Only Coach Brown stays behind. He waits until the room is cleared out before he shoves his hands in his pockets, clears his throat, and says, "Second-string coaching needs some adjustment."

My eyebrows shoot up into my hairline. "Okay, thanks for that feedback."

He nods and heads out the door.

At my desk, I look over the budget lines, head in my hands as I make notes. When I finally look up, I'm damn near cross-eyed as I call my assistant, Marielle, to ask her to set up a meeting with the finance team as soon as possible.

It's interesting to dig into the details of any organization. Some are a financial mess. Some are a morale mess. Some are a talent mess. This organization has good talent at the top. *"Second-string coaching needs some adjustment."* It wasn't that I was surprised to hear that, as that's clear, but I am thankful Coach Brown was willing to say it to me. That's the sort of coach a successful team keeps, because he is *all* about the team. The *whole* team. I don't want this A-plus team to crash and burn, and it's clear he doesn't either. *Good, because I can work with that.*

After a while, I just need a mental break, so I get up from my desk and head over to the window, which overlooks the city. There's so much information swimming around in my head that I realize I barely remember any of the names I learned on my tour around the building. I've heard that Bud Bellikowski was a good guy but perhaps absent. I don't want to be an absent GM. I want to get to know the staff and be part of the culture here.

Marielle pops her head in and asks if I'm interested in having her order me some lunch.

"You are a godsend," I say, stomach suddenly wide awake and rumbling. "That would be great. Can I just get a club sandwich and a side salad?"

"Easy," she says. Marielle is in her mid-forties. She's curvy, with a pleasant face, dirty-blonde hair piled on top of her head in a bun. "Anything else?"

"No, that will be plenty. Thanks so much."

She steps back out, and I hear her on the phone a moment later. While I wait for my food, I pull up the Crush website, making notes on places where I feel the fan experience might be enhanced. I find myself on the staff page, trying to connect the pictures and names to the people I met this morning.

As I make my way down the list, I come across Devon Pearson's photo. Team Nutritionist. God, she's gorgeous. And I'm a grade-A moron for being so cold and distant to her. I mean, I couldn't come out and be like, *Hey, Devon, last time we met, we were naked together in your hotel room.* But I also could've been nicer when Max introduced us. *Definitely could have been nicer.* Shit. I should go and apologize to her.

Just as I'm about to take a walk down to the lower level, Marielle comes in with my lunch.

"Marielle, how long have you been here?"

"Four years," she says. "I worked at one of the big hotels before this."

"Do you like it?"

"I love it. It's been a great place to work."

"Do you have family here?"

"Just my kids. My daughter is twelve and my son is ten," she says proudly.

"Oh, you have kids. Do they like hockey?"

"No," she says with a rueful smile. "My daughter is a dancer and my son plays baseball. No hockey players in the mix."

"Well, that's too bad."

She shrugs. "I let them do what they like. My late husband always talked about following your passions and I try to let them do that without much interference. It's worked pretty well so far."

"How did you lose your husband?"

"He died in a car accident. About five years ago. He worked for one of the big shows here in town and he was driving home late after a performance and got broadsided by a drunk driver."

"Whoa, that's terrible. I'm so sorry."

"It was hard but we're okay. Thanks for asking about me, though."

"Well, it's good to know about your colleagues, I think."

"You'll fit in well here," she says. "This place is a family."

"So I've heard."

As Marielle heads toward the door, I add, "Thanks again for grabbing lunch."

"It's my job. Let me know if you need anything else."

Devon Pearson.

I don't say it, of course, but it's there. *She* is what I'd love Marielle to get for me, because *she* is delicious. Every fucking beautiful curve and line of her.

And sadly, I'll never get another taste.

Working with her here might be harder than I thought.

14
probably just anxiety

Devon

Hardly anyone is around since it's summertime, certainly not many of our players, so I pack it in early, needing a break from the stifling reality that a man I've had hot sex with is now working in my building.

Before I even get to the door of my own apartment, I stop at Gia's and bang on the door. She opens up, saying, "Look at you, breaking the law."

I must look confused because she adds, "You left work early, Dev."

"Oh, yeah," I say. "Had a hard time concentrating today."

"Because that hot stud was walking around making you squirm?"

"Yep." I nod, my lips pushed together. "Yeppers. That was distracting."

"Did you guys have a chance to discuss...things?" Gia asks coyly.

"No. Nope, stayed far away from the administrative offices today. Today and all days henceforth."

"Don't be silly, you're going to have to figure out how to deal with it. He's the GM now."

"Thanks for the reminder, I think I've mostly processed this fact by now, Gia." I'm cranky and emotionally exhausted and not inclined to hide it with my best friend.

She just laughs and says, "Well, I know what you need, so go get changed into running clothes and we'll take it out on the pavement."

I let a big sigh out through my nose and nod. "Okay. Yep. Fine."

Ten minutes later, I'm back at her door, dressed to run.

As we head out, Gia asks if I've told anyone else about my hot night with a sexy stranger.

"No! Of course, I haven't. Who else would I tell?"

"Any of your friends at work?"

"Absolutely not. Those are work friends and I don't talk to them about my sex life."

"Or lack thereof." Gia cackles.

My friend is brash and loud and says things I would never say. I'm too reserved, too afraid of rocking the boat. I look over at her as we run and grin to myself. She's petite, maybe five three on the high side, with a short, blonde pixie cut. She's in a ripped-up, off-the-shoulder T-shirt for some '90s band and a pair of ultra-short athletic shorts. She looks like a punk-rock co-ed and not at all like the up-and-coming UNLV professor that she is.

"How's summer session?" I ask, changing the subject away from my sex life.

"Fine," she says. "I'm teaching three freshman-level science classes, so I have the kids who are making up credits, or who forgot to take something and need it to graduate. But it's cool."

"How's the crusty old department chair? Doctor…"

"Dr. Rubenstein," she says, making a face. "Blech. Dr. Frankenstein, more like. Crusty old bastard."

"Still giving you the grunt work, huh?"

"It's all politics. Earn your keep and whatnot. He won't be around forever."

We run for a little while in silence before a thought occurs to me. "Hey, did you sleep with Mikhail?"

All I get is a shining, wide smile in return.

"So that's a yes." Geesh. "I guess I should have warned you to maybe not sleep with my coworkers?"

"Pish."

"Dude, seriously."

"I fail to see how my sleeping with a Crush player has any bearing on your ability to assure his nutritional well-being," she answers firmly. "And also, all those hamburgers are not making their way onto that body. He is pure muscle. Yum."

"Gross."

"No, ma'am. Not gross. Delicious and tasty."

"La-la-la-la-la-la," I sing, putting my fingers in my ears. "Not interested."

"You're the one who asked."

She's not wrong, so I let it go. I'm not all that worried, as Gia has a very short attention span, and a very low tolerance for feelings. A hockey player is actually probably perfect for her in that way. She'll lose interest soon enough.

Me, on the other hand? Can't stop thinking about the guy I can't have. Still interested. Very, very interested.

This is not good news for me.

"You look like you're constipated over there," Gia says, giggling. "You need to do a poop-run?"

I laugh at this. "No. I'm good. Just thinking about Grant Gerard."

"And it makes your face do that?"

"Only when I'm thinking about how unfunny it is that I've seen that man very, very naked and now I have to be professional around him every day."

"Well, think of him, poor guy. He's got to be professional around you *and* be the big boss, when he's been *way far* inside of you."

I feel a flush across my chest that has nothing to do with the fact that we've now run two miles. I remember just how far inside of me he was. I can only groan in response.

"Let's be honest. You'll probably only see him once

every six months or something, based on your interactions with the last GM, right?"

"Maybe?"

"Likely," Gia corrects. "You'll never see him. No big deal."

"I just hate that I threw caution to the wind one time. One time I let myself toss my inhibitions and just go for it and now it's a big mess."

"Don't be such a drama queen, Dev. It's not that big of a mess. You're an adult. He's an adult. You were both consenting, and you didn't work together when it happened. I'm sure today was a shock for you both but, you'll both also get over it."

"I guess that's a good point."

"Of course, it is. I have a PhD," Gia says. "Plus, you're out of there in a year. Once your cookbook and business take off, you won't have to work there anymore anyway. So just focus on that and move up the timeline if things get too weird."

"Yeah," I say, feeling more hopeful. "You're right. I can do this for a limited time. I'll just focus on the work, and I'll get the business off the ground. I'll finish the book. I'll hide out in my dungeon closet office, and I'll probably never see the guy. It will be fine."

"That's the spirit!" Gia high-fives me as we continue to run. After a moment, she adds, "It is a sad thing though."

"What?"

"Having to ignore a guy that hot."

"You're not wrong. I've never dated anyone like him. He's the whole package. Funny, interesting, smart, attractive, great in bed." I throw my head back and let out a weird, animal sound of frustration. "Figures he's off-limits."

"Does he have to be?"

"I mean…other people have obviously found each other and worked together there. The non-fraternization policy is pretty much a joke at this point, but he doesn't need to be seen as the GM who starts screwing the employees the minute he starts the job. For that matter, what would they think of *me*?"

"I guess you're right about that."

The longer we run, the more I start to feel a little off, my stomach souring. I'm obviously not used to running at this time of day. *Maybe we should have run at the normal knock-off time.* "Hey, can we turn back? I'm not feeling well."

"You getting sick?"

I shake my head. "No, probably just anxiety from this very weird day. I was just thinking it could be because we're running two hours earlier than we normally do, too."

"Makes sense."

We make it back and Gia puts her head on my shoulder before opening her apartment door. "Feel better, mama. Get some rest and let me know if you need some chicken soup or something."

"Thanks, friend."

After showering and putting on my favorite pajamas, I'm feeling much better, so I head into the kitchen, determined to work on the cookbook recipes. I'm able to focus for about an hour, taste-testing a grilled chicken and tangerine salad that will double for my dinner. It's a winner and will definitely make the cut for the cookbook, so I take a bunch of pictures while it looks pretty on the plate. But throughout this process, my mind keeps wandering back to Grant.

Always back to Grant, if I'm being honest. Why does the first man I'm deeply attracted to have to be the one I simply can't have?

My memories of our night together are vivid in my mind. Every minute of our encounter is imprinted. Sometimes I feel like I can still smell him, his masculine and woodsy scent. I can still feel his dark hair in my hands as he shoved his tongue inside of me. I can still taste his mouth and feel his thrusts deep inside me. I can remember how it felt having his cock in my mouth when he came the second time down my throat. We got around to some of everything in our short time together.

Getting a little wet and hot between the legs, I have to stop what I'm doing in the kitchen. I go straight for the nightstand drawer and the tiny, pink toy that awaits. I fire it up and crawl under my covers, using one hand to push my pussy lips apart to expose my clit to the vibrating treasure ready to go to work on me. I turn it on and fall into the sensations, its pulsations causing my hips to rise, my muscles to tense.

You're so fucking gorgeous, Devon, taking my cock. Come for me. Come all over my fuckin' cock right now! It doesn't take long. Just a few minutes of remembering the sex with Grant and I'm over the edge, coming ridiculously fast to the memories of my night with a man I cannot forget.

15
a business dinner

Grant

It's early enough that I figure she won't yet be there. I'm such a pussy that I'm walking to her office at a time when I don't actually expect her to be in. Because if she's not there, then I can just leave a note and tell her I'm sorry I've been such a dick. I won't have to look her in the eyes and explain why it's taken me two full weeks to come back down here to see her and apologize.

Two weeks since I started this job. Two weeks since I acted like a cold, uncaring bastard.

I'd blame it on being busy, but I could've made it happen.

When I get to Devon's office, the lights are on, but she's not around. Good, I guess. I grab a pen and a Post-it, write a note, and stick it to her monitor.

HEY,

SORRY I WAS AN ASS.
LET'S TALK SOMETIME.
GG

Her computer is powered on, which means she's around in the building somewhere. Maybe I should just wait for her.

The big pussy in me opts to duck out, but as I walk out into the hall, I see her emerging from the ladies' room. She looks surprised to see me, her eyes going wide, but her hand is holding her stomach, and her skin tone looks a little off-color. Kind of greenish.

"Hey, you okay?"

She gives me a weak smile. "Just been a little off the past few days. A virus or something, maybe."

"Have you seen a doctor?"

"No, too busy."

"Oh, are we sending too many clients your way, or—"

She laughs softly and shakes her head at me.

"No, not at all. I don't think I've told you that I have a whole side gig. I'm writing a cookbook and I also run a small nutrition consultancy and cooking school. There's too much to do, no time to be sick."

"Well, rest helps. Can you take a few days off and recuperate? Maybe you're just running yourself too thin?"

"Maybe," she says. "It's slow here right now, with

so few players around. I could maybe take a day off this week.”

“Well, you have my permission, if it helps any.” I flash her a smile.

Devon looks unimpressed.

“I, uh, actually came down here to find you.” The need to explain myself to this woman is real. It may be a new experience for me to be doing this, but still something I can’t put off any longer. “I wanted to apologize…for that first day. I was really caught off guard seeing you working here, and I didn’t know how to play it. I panicked. It was so stupid, and I feel like a fuckin’ ass, but for what it’s worth, I’m really sorry.”

“Oh gosh,” she answers, straightening her posture and pulling her hair back in a long ponytail. Her color has improved a little in these few moments we’ve been talking. “It’s no big deal. I totally get it. New job, lots to learn. You weren’t expecting to run into someone you recognized.”

“Or, specifically, someone I’d been intimate with.” My voice is almost husky as I say this. Goddamn, why can’t I control myself in her presence? I quickly add, “I guess you could say I’m ripping the Band-Aid right off with this.”

She blushes and it’s maybe the prettiest thing I’ve seen in a while. “Yeah, well, that is the truth of it, right? It is awkward.”

“It doesn’t have to be, though. That night was—”

"In the past, Grant."

I bite the inside of my lip as I consider her. She's giving me an out. What's in the past can stay in the past. No harm, no foul. No reliving it—even as good as it was. Even though I want to. Many times.

But she's right—even about what she's not saying out loud. Which is: we need to be professional and work together as colleagues only.

As if reading my mind, she says, "You're the new GM. You don't need rumors swirling around about you. Not about stuff like this. I can't risk my job either."

I give a short nod. "Sure, right. Of course."

"Okay, then we're good. All is well." Devon starts to turn away, heading for her office. "It was good to see you. I do appreciate the apology."

As she walks away, I can't stop myself from adding, "Hey, Devon?"

She turns, one perfectly shaped eyebrow arched in question.

"Would you want to go to dinner with me tonight?" When I see her mouth open in protest, brows furrowed, I rush to add, "Nothing inappropriate. I just don't know anyone here. I could use a friend and I also want to pick your brain about the team and your approach to nutrition with them."

"A business dinner?"

"A business dinner. That's all. Nothing more than that."

"Okay," she says after a moment.

"Awesome. I'll swing down here around five? You can pick the place."

She nods and turns away again. I watch her for a moment before heading my own way, resisting the urge to turn myself right back around to see her again.

ALL DAY I AM DISTRACTED.

I keep having to stop my knee from bouncing. Or having to bring my focus back online after my attention wanders to a certain employee working several floors below me.

I have now come to terms with the fact that this "business dinner" was merely a ruse.

Just a way for me to get to spend some time with Devon Pearson.

I've felt the pull every day I've been here. Every fucking day for two weeks, I've wanted to go talk to her and explain my actions. For two long weeks, I've longed to ask her to forgive me for being a heartless prick when we were introduced.

And she just let me off the hook for all of it.

Said it was *no big deal.*

Understood why I behaved the way I did.

Wasn't mad.

And I believe that she's telling me the truth.

Fuck me sideways.

I know I *should* just walk away from this potential drama. I know I *should* keep things ultra-professional with Devon on those rare occasions our paths might cross. I know it would be best for me to just leave things alone and in the past where they *should* stay. Of course, I know all of this and what I *should* be doing where Devon is concerned.

The problem is my "little brain" has no interest in listening to what I *should* be doing, nor listening to the bigger and more logical brain residing behind my skull.

My dick doesn't fucking care. I do know that much.

It wants Devon Pearson again on any terms it might have her.

It's possible I've made a huge mistake by inviting her to dinner. *But right now, I don't fucking care, either.*

16
the library

At a quarter to five, I get up from my desk and stretch. I feel much better than I did earlier and am actually kind of hungry now. I take a few minutes to finish up some work, then run a brush through my hair and retie my ponytail. I put on some lip gloss and as soon as I put it back in my purse, Grant is at my office door, giving me a smile that nearly stops my heart.

"How was your day?" he asks.

I can hardly form words to answer; he's so sexy in his dark suit and dress shirt, unbuttoned at the top. I manage to squeak out a tiny, "It was fine. Slow."

"You feeling any better?"

"I am. Thank you. But if you're uncomfortable, we can take a raincheck. I don't want you getting sick or anything."

"Oh, I'm not worried," Grant answers. "I have,

like, iron-strong immunity. People around me could be dropping like flies, but I just hardly ever get sick." He knocks on the wooden doorjamb.

"Okay, then. Because I'm famished. What kind of food do you like?"

"I'm kind of a dude," he answers. Or non-answers, I suppose.

"And what does that mean, exactly?"

With a chuckle, he tilts his head at me. "I'm a meat and potatoes kind of guy."

"Well, I know just the place, then. It's usually not too busy at this early hour and the food is great. Total hidden gem in a town where restaurants are always flooded with tourists. Also, we're going to talk about getting you a more adventurous nutritional plan."

"Hey, you're off the clock," he says, a panty-dropping, lopsided smile nearly making me weak in the knees. His *dimple*. I forgot about that.

"Nope." I fold my arms over my chest. "I *am* on the clock. You said this was a business dinner and that we'd talk about nutrition for the team. You're part of the extended team, so..."

Another laugh, and then he nods at me. "Well, then, I am open to being schooled. Shall we?"

I take his proffered elbow, a sharp current shooting through me as I do, the hint of want growing inside me the closer I get to him. It's probably a good thing the restaurant I suggested for dinner is an easy walking distance from the offices. Some fresh air and a brisk walk might help to clear away all the illegal thoughts running through my head whenever Grant Gerard is within smelling distance.

Of course, he smells amazing during our entire stroll over to the restaurant, fresh air and all, with his woodsy, spiced cologne or whatever delicious scent it is he wears with the power to whip my hormones into a lusty frenzy every damn time he's near. Is it going to be this much of a struggle controlling myself around him? Good God. *We're just walking. And I'm feeling aroused already. I'm so screwed here.*

We don't say much during our walk. Strangely, the vibe between us doesn't feel at all awkward—beyond my irrational desire to climb him like a tree. It's a comfortable silence between us. I don't ever remember feeling that way on a date before.

This is not a date, it's a business dinner like Grant said.

"Here we are," I tell him, pointing to the door of our destination.

"The Library, huh?" He holds the door and ushers me inside.

"Do you know it?"

"No, but it looks like we've just stepped inside an old-world library, so their name is on point." Grant takes charge of speaking to the hostess and getting us seated in a comfortable corner nook, shelves all around us filled with gorgeous leather-bound books that must be worth a fortune. I always enjoy studying the titles of books on literally every topic whenever I've eaten here.

"If you're a meat and potatoes guy, then I think you'll find something you like here."

"I know I will." Something about the way he just said, *I know I will,* suggests he's not talking about the food, even though he's focusing on his menu. Without looking up, he says, "This looks perfect, Devon. Thank you for agreeing to have dinner with me."

"Of c-course, I'm h-happy to." I cringe inwardly. Why did I just stumble over my words like that? *Idiot!* I bury my face in my menu and read that shit like it's the latest from George R. R. Martin hot off the presses.

After a moment, he casually asks if I'd like him to order some wine to go with our dinner.

"No, I don't think that's a great idea." I feel heat start spreading up my neck.

When I look up from my menu, it's to find him staring. Our eyes meet and hold for a beat or two. I swear, his hazel eyes darken as we study each other. The last time we drank together, well, things got crazy…

"Fair enough," he says with the merest smile, shaking free of what I would guess is the same memory I've been replaying since he started working here.

After our orders are in, a steak for Grant, and roasted chicken for me, he asks how I work with the trainers and physical therapy teams to do my job.

"Well, I talk to Dale a lot. He's the main strength trainer; did you meet him?"

A shake of the head.

"He's goofy, and he's been known to hit on all the single women who work for the Crush, but I think he's a good trainer."

My new sort-of boss cringes at this. "Do I need to worry about this guy hitting on his colleagues? My first HR visit?"

"No, he's harmless. He flirts but he's never crossed a line."

There's a thick silence between us that speaks volumes. What happened between us is still so vivid for me, and by the way he looks at me, I think it must be for him. I'm thankful when our salads arrive, giving us a minute to focus on something else. Still, he did ask me a question, and I need to get back to the business part of our "business dinner."

"I was saying that I work closely with Dale. Really, he's the one I coordinate with. He does a lot of group and individual strength training, but he's also pretty open to collaboration. He did some group stretching classes with Pam in PT. He's sent some of the team to my nutrition and cooking classes. We talk often about guys who need a little more support in different areas."

Grant listens and asks questions about the players' nutritional needs. He's attentive and inquisitive, which I appreciate. He talks about the pragmatic side of things—we pay these guys a lot of money. They need to be in top physical shape. He's concerned that the second- and third-string guys aren't getting as much attention as the top guys.

"I suppose that might be true, but they're all different. They've all been required to log some serious time in the gym and with me, but some of them value it more than others. That goes for the big guys, too. They're inconsistent, really. I feel like there's a point at which they come to it on their own, you know? They realize they need to let off the partying throttle a bit, get more serious about their physicality. They mature, grow up, and get serious. Some of these guys are teenagers still, or not far past it when they land at the NHL level, and not thinking much beyond what to have for dinner, let alone a whole nutritional plan."

"I do know about that," Grant says. "I didn't get serious about my body and how I treated it until I got tapped for the Olympic team. I thought I could live like a college student forever. Not true."

This makes me smile. "Many of our guys view the experience as a fraternity, I think."

"Well, that's not a totally bad thing. I keep hearing over and over that the place is like a family."

"It is, for some."

"Not for you?"

"I enjoy it. I care about the players and my team of

coworkers a great deal. But I try to keep work and life separate."

"I get that. How did you end up working for the Crush? How long have you been here?"

"I've worked for the team for four years. Moved to Vegas for the job. Well, also to get as far away from my ex-husband as possible."

"You were married?" Grant seems genuinely surprised.

"I was. He was a pro basketball player. Played in Miami and then New York. We met in college, got married right away, and stayed married four years."

"What happened? Just too young?"

I raise a shoulder. "Maybe that. It was… tumultuous. It was better for my sanity to get out of the relationship and put as many miles between us as possible."

Grant is nodding vigorously. "I feel that. I think I mentioned I was married too? Our divorce was final six months ago, but honestly, it was over long before that. And walking in on her, naked, with my good friend in our bed didn't help."

"Ugh," I groan. I cannot believe anyone would cheat on Grant. Not only is he such a nice guy, but he's great-looking and spectacular in bed. *What was wrong with her to decide to cheat on* him? Although, perhaps I know the answer to that. Shawn was remarkably selfish and often self-absorbed, so my bet is that Grant's ex was also. "My ex cheated, too, which was the final blow. Things were good and then they were terrible. And then they were good. And then they were terrible. It was emotional whiplash, all the time with him. I feel so much better and healthier now than I ever felt when I was with Shawn."

"I get that. Things with Margot, my ex, were good for a long time. We tried having a baby and just couldn't get pregnant. We tried and tried, and it only created this wedge between us. I really wanted a family, and she wasn't as keen about it. But, irony of all irony, she's pregnant now. It happened really fast for her in her new relationship. In hindsight, it's good it didn't happen. Sharing a child would be hard now since things ended."

I can tell he's really disappointed about not having kids. I can totally see Grant as a father. He's funny and warm and smart. He'd probably be a very hands-on dad. I don't say any of that, of course. I just say, "I agree, splitting is easier when there are no kids involved. It's probably a blessing in disguise that it never happened for the two of you."

"Well, we've both been through the ringer, I suppose. But we survived. And I'm happy to get started somewhere new."

I nod and focus on the last of my dinner for a moment, mulling a question I know I shouldn't ask. Still, I can't help myself. "So, have you dated much since your divorce?"

I want him to say no. I want to be the only one he's

been with, the only one who's caught his attention. I know I shouldn't care. I can't have him anyway, not now that we work together. But still.

"No, not at all...well, except for meeting you that night." He nails me with another golden stare touched with the remembrance of our wild time together, no doubt. I let out the breath I didn't realize I was holding, the butterflies fluttering inside my stomach. "I'm not sure how it all works, honestly. I've been out of the game for a while."

I nod. "I get that."

"How about you?"

"Um, I date every once in a while, but no one has really made my toes curl since my divorce." *Until you.* I don't say that part, but it hangs in the air between us as our eyes meet. Again, a ghost of a smile tilts the corners of his mouth. Ugh, his gorgeous mouth.

He works his teeth over his bottom lip, and my nipples go hard, a chill running through me as I think about those teeth grazing against my skin. I know his thoughts have gone there, too, when his eyes darken again, and he adjusts his position in his chair.

"What we did together..." He trails off, his eyes never leaving mine.

"We can't pretend it didn't happen," I suggest. Grant opens his mouth to speak, but I shake my head, stopping him. The words spill out of me like marbles from a bag, rolling across the table, hard to control. "We didn't know we'd be working together, and we didn't do anything wrong. But it can't happen again, obviously. I mean, I know this must be so awkward for you, as the new GM, and I'm not here to make life difficult for you. I get where you're at with this job and I want you to be successful. I'm not expecting anything from you."

Grant is the one shaking his head now—vigorously. "I don't want to pretend it didn't happen, Devon. I've thought about you every single day since. I wanted to call, but it seemed pointless. I figured you lived in, like, Ohio or something. It never even occurred to me you lived here. It felt like something that wouldn't be able to work. But I've thought about you. I don't know what made me walk over and talk to you, but I'm so very glad I did. I don't regret a thing about meeting you that night."

I should not say it, but of course, I do. "I've thought about you every day, too."

We stare some more at each other for a few long seconds, my toes definitely curling in my shoes as I push my knees together, futile in my attempt to dampen the wanton ache I feel between my legs. I can hardly breathe, looking at him.

"I don't know what this is, Devon," he says, nearly growling the words at me. "I want to explore it further, but it would have to be on the down-low. I hate that, but you understand why. For now, at least."

"I do understand." It comes out quiet, timid sounding even. I have to take a breath and let it out so that I can continue speaking. "I'm not into being someone's secret, though. And please don't forget, I have a job to protect, too."

"You shouldn't have to be someone's secret," he says, his fingers drumming wildly on the table. There's a nervous, animal energy around him now. He looks like he would pounce if he thought it was safe to do so. "You're beautiful. Smart. Your body is perfection. You deserve to be worshipped, openly, and I can't...*I hate* that it can't be me. Because, Devon, I fucking want you. So badly."

Oh God. God, I want him too.

The electricity between us is a steady current now. It was there on the night we spent together, for sure, but different. New. Exciting. Out of my comfort zone. Now? It's pure, unadulterated lust.

I want him.

He wants me. *"Because, Devon, I fucking want you."*

He's off-limits, though.

I *should* thank him for dinner, ignoring the heat and ache between my legs.

I *should* wish him luck and remind him of the necessary boundaries.

I *should* walk away, returning to my quiet home.

I *should* do all of these things, but I can't.

And then he answers for me by catching our server by the arm, his voice husky and determined as he says, "Check, please."

17
just a secret for a little while

Grant

My hand is pressed low at Devon's back as I whisk her from the restaurant and into an awaiting cab. She blurts out her address quickly, something I barely register against the backdrop of my thundering heartbeat. My cock has been semi-hard for about three-fourths of the evening so far. With Devon's luscious beauty, something my body cannot ignore, in spite of my valiant efforts to tamp it down, the little brain between my legs is driving the bus now.

We're both silent on the ride, Devon's chest rising and falling as she works to control her breathing. There's no doubt we're both feeling this. The air between us is thick and heavy, almost suffocating. I want to shove up her skirt and then pull her to my lap and right onto my cock. I want her writhing and moaning as we fuck in the back seat of this cab, and I couldn't care less if the driver were to witness.

The best I can do, though, is put my hand on the seat between us, fingers spread wide so that my pinky touches her leg. I move it ever so slightly, just enough to feel the softness where her skirt has ridden up and exposed creamy skin.

When we stop, I throw some money up into the front seat and help Devon out to the sidewalk. We head inside a nondescript apartment building I couldn't describe to anyone if they asked. I have no idea where we even are in this city. Minor details to where my head is at right now.

Into the elevator. Up three floors. Four doors down a long hallway.

It's a blur. Each step is a step closer, but still too far away. She fumbles with her keys, struggling to get the lock open. Pulling me inside, she slams the door, locks it, and gives me a look of near madness.

"Grant, I want to—I mean we shouldn't, but—"

I lean forward, put my hand to the back of her head, and pull her lips to mine. Conversation time is over. I can only think of all the dirty things I want to do to her.

She sighs the instant our lips meet, opening her mouth for me, our tongues tangling as I press in deep to claim more of the kisses haunting me relentlessly ever since our night together. Pushing up her skirt with my free hand, I slide right in between her legs to feel how wet she is already. *Oh yeah.* Fingers dip beneath the edge of silky panties and sink into her slick heat. She moans against my mouth as I make contact, then arching onto my fingers, starting to fuck her with a singular purpose in mind.

Making her come right here, right now on my hand, while pinned against the door of her apartment because we can't wait the extra minute of time it would take to make it to a bed.

This beautiful woman in my arms needs to come with my fingers in her cunt and my tongue in her mouth.

She needs it. I need to give it to her.

While I work on making her come, she works on loosening my belt, unzipping my pants, and stroking over my cock through my shorts. Just having her hands on me feels...fucking incredible. This woman is incredible.

Somehow, we're moving, kissing, touching each other as we get busy with getting naked at the same time. We pull away our layers—blouse, shirt, pants, skirt, shoes, socks. She unhooks her bra, her beautiful breasts spilling out for me to lick. I take my fingers out of her pussy to get her panties down her legs and off.

A pity, that.

But I have plans to make up for it. Very. Very. Soon.

I look around wildly and figure her kitchen table will just have to do for what I have in mind.

Picking her up, I bring her over to the surface and sit her down. Pushing her legs apart, I dive between them, my tongue eager and exploring. My thumb works her clit as my tongue sinks inside her tight heat. She pulls at my hair, pushing me to partake, to devour her, to gorge myself on her beautiful, beautiful body.

She makes sexy sounds that could make me come just from hearing her. When I think I might, I stand and take a breath, my vision slightly blurry. I feel drugged. I feel out of control. And she looks the same, her gaze unfocused, her hair wild around her shoulders as she grips the side of the table, her pussy wet and swollen, ready to be fucked by me.

I lower my boxers, my cock so hard it could probably function as a glass cutter in a pinch. I hear myself ask her what she wants. I swear I could be having an out-of-body experience from how blurred by lust I am right now.

"I want to ride you," she says, licking her lips in a way that makes the tip of my cock seep with the need to be in her.

I nod, holding out my hand to help her from the table down to the floor. She steps gingerly, like her legs have gone weak, but she still pushes me to the floor with a strength that's impressive. The floor is hardwood, cold and unforgiving, but I couldn't care less. I doubt she cares either. All I can think about is getting my cock inside her.

She helps me find a condom in the pocket of my rumpled pants and then eagerly rolls it onto my bobbing cock. It's pure perfection when she straddles me before sinking her warm, wet cunt down onto my cock. We both cry out from how good it feels. She proceeds to ride me as requested, hands on my chest, fingernails biting down into my skin. I can't stop touching her—her ass, hips, thighs, the soft skin of her lower back. I lean up and take one erect nipple into my mouth, biting and sucking and teasing as she throws her head back, arches her back toward me, soft sounds of satisfaction coming from deep in her throat.

One tit satisfied, I move to the other, and when I do, she starts to come, her walls tightening around my cock. Her cunt pulses and pulses as she thrashes her head wildly, the noises coming out of her intense and animalistic and nonsensical.

Only when she seems to settle do I sit up, holding her against me, standing us up. Still connected, I walk to the living room, to the carpeted floor. I put her down on her back, slipping loose as she cries out in protest, "No!"

"I know," I say, repositioning myself. I kiss her, look into her fever-bright eyes. I kiss her flushed cheeks and her perfect tits. When I sink back into her, she bends her legs, giving me deeper access. I push those long legs up, folding them over my shoulders. It feels like we're one person.

"So deep," I groan as I start to fuck her in earnest, my thrusts growing faster, harder, more desperate.

"More," she pleads. "Please...don't ever stop."

I won't, baby. In and out, I push harder, each moment closer.

She closes her eyes and turns her head to the side as her pussy begins to clench around me again. "No," I scold. "I want your eyes looking at me when you come."

The way she looks up at me? So responsive following my command to perfection? It makes my balls tighten with the impending explosion. My own orgasm starts and overtakes everything else. Her pussy clenches so hard around me, over and over, squeezing me dry, taking from me. I empty into her with a roar, not letting up until I feel her relax and her body go boneless.

We lie there together for a long time, me on top of her, my cock still twitching inside of her, her breathing labored, her hand slowly stroking my back. I don't know how much time passes, but eventually, I get up, helping her to her feet. She heads into the bathroom, and I clean up in the kitchen before going back to find her.

She emerges, still looking slightly dazed, and crawls onto her bed, patting the space beside her. I don't need a second invitation. Naked, we lie on top of her comforter, just breathing and recovering. *Fucking hell. She's...she's just incredible.* Sex with her is unworldly. Extraordinary. I nod off for a moment, and maybe she does too.

After a long time, we turn and face each other. I run my fingertips down her side, reveling at the way it makes her skin erupt in gooseflesh. "I don't think I can stay away from you, Devon," I finally say, my voice dry and hoarse all of a sudden. "It's not just the sex, which is enough, believe me. I just really like you. A lot. Being in your company. I like talking to you, and I can really use a friend in a new city."

Devon is quiet for a long minute, her eyes seemingly focused on my lips. When she refocuses to meet my gaze, she says, "I've been working on launching my own business, you know. I'm testing out the model right now. Trying some new things. Getting the cookbook together. If things work, this could be my last season with the Crush before I set out on my own."

"I'm not sure what you're telling me," I confess.

"I'm saying..." She stops talking. Takes a breath. "I'm not big on being someone's secret, Grant, but I want you to be successful here. So maybe it's just a secret for a little while. One season, and then I can set out on my own and we'll be free to see each other openly."

I put my hand on her cheek and lean in for a kiss. "Let's take it day by day, beautiful, gorgeous Devon. I need you to know I'd be proud to have you on my arm, yeah? In my bed. At my side. But I appreciate your discretion right now. I promise I won't take it for granted."

She answers by pushing me to my back, her mouth on my pectorals, my stomach…

And then my cock.

18
we did talk about business

Devon

I wake up disoriented and sore, confused by the beeping that turns out to be my alarm clock. Fumbling for the snooze, I lie back down, trying to get my brain to work.

Grant was here until after midnight. He left regretfully, apologizing, saying he wished he could stay. I kissed him all the way to the door, watching him slip out into the night before padding back to bed and falling into one of the deepest sleeps of my life.

When the alarm goes off again, I force myself up and into my running clothes. I'll have to Uber to work today because my car is still in the Crush parking structure where I parked it *yesterday morning*. Christ. We were so desperate to be together, both of us just abandoned our cars there to come here...and come.

I have no idea if Grant took a cab back to the offices after he left here to collect his car or just went home. I can only pray nobody at work catches on to the fact that both of our vehicles were parked there into the wee hours of the morning.

For a solid two miles, I manage to focus only on my gait, my steps, the movement of my arms, and my breathing. But then the panic sets in. *This is not a good idea.* Secretly sleeping with the new GM? I am an idiot. Why did I let that happen? *How* could I let it happen?

It was just supposed to be dinner. A business dinner. And yes, we talked about work, but that spark simply grew and grew until it threatened to set the table on fire.

No alcohol involved this time.

This is no fluke, this *thing* with Grant.

And the sex?

Oh my, glorious, God.

So, good.

Like, it's making me blush out here on my morning run just remembering it, kind of good.

But...the flutters of anxiety are definitely present. The flip of my stomach. My heartbeat out of control. My fuzzy head and the feeling that I might pass out right here on the street. I slow my run to a jog, then a walk as my skin goes cold and clammy. I stop, crouching, head between my legs as I throw up. Right there beside the sidewalk, I toss my cookies into the dirt, a full-blown panic attack fully achieved.

Go me.

Unable to run any farther, I text Gia, telling her what just happened. When I get home, I'm tired and anxious, still feeling nauseated. This viral bug is the worst and so unpredictable. Thankfully, Gia meets me at the door to my apartment, putting her hand on my forehead like some old auntie taking my temperature.

"You don't feel like you have a fever," she crows as we head inside. Straight to the refrigerator, she grabs a seltzer water and tips some into a glass as I flop onto the couch, exhausted.

"What's up with you, friend?" she asks, handing me the cold drink.

I hold the cool glass to my forehead for a moment before finally taking a sip, the carbonation instantly calming my stomach. "I'm a stupid idiot."

"There are words I might use to describe you, Dev, but *stupid* and *idiot* are not among them. I'll need more explanation, please."

"I slept with him again."

Gia's face mashes in confusion at first, but then it dawns on her. "Oh. Oh! Hottie guy from the hotel."

I nod, tipping my head back against the couch cushions. "Grant Gerard. Newly hired GM of the Crush. My employer."

"How did that happen?" Gia asks before adding, "I mean, I know how sex happens. I meant, how did you end up in his orbit in that particular way?"

"I hadn't seen him in like two weeks. He came down yesterday morning to say he was sorry for being cold or whatever at our introduction. I let him off the hook because, frankly, we can't be screwing around like this. But then he said he needed a friend and asked me to a business dinner. And I said yes."

"To a business dinner." Gia's tone is flat.

"Yes. And we did talk about business."

"But."

"But." I sigh. "He's hot. And there's this—*thing*—between us."

"Some might call that his erect penis," my friend says with a laugh, earning the side-eye from me.

"Well, Gia, it is rather magnificent, as penises go. Big, talented, endlessly powerful." I throw my hands up in defeat. "Chemistry, my dear. Seriously. Too much chemistry between us to fight it a moment longer. It was like I was suffocating from the need for sex...with *him*."

"Wow." She sounds impressed. "I don't think I've ever seen you toot someone's horn quite like that. Congratulations."

"No. Not congratulations, Gia. This is not good. I can't be sleeping with the new GM. It will get us both fired. I can't have every attempt at a perfectly professional working relationship go sideways when he looks at me with those gorgeous hazel eyes of his."

"Like, literally sideways," she says with a snort.

"You're not helping."

"Sorry, not sorry. So, you were having dinner and you got all hot and bothered..."

Another sigh from me. "And we ended up here and it was like we were both under the influence of some otherworldly sexual power or something. And it was absolutely amazing. I really, really like him, Gia. Grant Gerard is a lovely man."

"Well, shit."

"Ya think?"

"What are you going to do?"

I throw my hands up. "I don't know. I guess I'm his secret sex bunny now or something. Because neither of us wants to stay away, but we can't really be public about it while we work at the same place."

Gia sniggers. "Secret sex bunny is also not a term I'd have ever associated with you, Dev. Who are you and what have you done with my introverted, rule-following friend?"

"Maybe I can get the business launched earlier than next summer. Or we can just sneak around for the season. I don't know."

"Well, take it day by day. I mean, I've had great sex with guys who turned out to be total turds. Don't put this guy on a pedestal just because he's the first guy to rev your engine in a while."

"It's not like that though. He's a good guy."

"Still, you've known him for like two minutes. Get to know him. Take it slow. No need to go public while you're just learning about each other anyway."

"You're probably right. I'm jumping the gun. If things get serious, I guess we'll figure that out when and if it comes." I take another sip of my drink and then rub the side of the cool glass against my forehead.

Gia asks, "You feeling any better? You're not pregnant, are you?"

My stomach sinks as I remember the weird condom issue on the night we met. But he said he couldn't get his wife pregnant, even though they tried for a long time. "No. I mean, I've been feeling really crummy lately, but I'm sure it's just nerves about Grant and the side business and whatnot. I've had anxiety before. This feels like anxiety."

"Well, you might want to invest in some heavy-duty birth control. That guy looks like he could get you pregnant by just smiling at you."

I laugh and force myself up. "I've got to get ready for work. Thanks for taking care of me."

"Anytime, chump," she says, heading to the door. "I'll check in later tonight."

I try to put it out of my mind, but as my stomach crawls with nausea all through my shower, I can't stop thinking about the broken condom and the man who said he couldn't get anyone pregnant. His ex got pregnant quickly with her new boyfriend, right? That's what he said. So that proves I can't be pregnant because he can't get anyone pregnant.

It's probably fine, right?

19

tell me about devon's class

Grant

"Isn't he camera-ready, girls? Phew," says Scarlett, fanning herself with her hands. "I need to send Vik to your tailor just to get him in a suit that fits this well."

I shake my head, grinning. "He's a big guy. Probably needs a custom tailor anyway. It's hard to buy a nice suit off the rack anytime, but when you're as tall and broad as he is? No chance he's looking good in something off the rack."

"When does Viktor wear a suit, though?" Ella, one of Scarlett's PR coordinators, says. "Besides game days and press events?"

Scarlett's sigh is dramatic. "We never go out anymore. Especially since we found out about baby number two, it's just been so hard to plan for anything more than a quick bite to eat. What I wouldn't give for a fancy dinner out, or a romantic weekend in the mountains or at the beach."

"It's hard to connect when you have little ones," Ella says as she rolls nearly undetectable lint from the back of my suit jacket. "I remember when Cedric and I had Britni, we didn't go out for five years."

"Five years," Scarlett cries. "No. I refuse to let this go on for that long."

"So how is parenthood?" I ask her as the photographer takes a few test shots to check lighting.

"Oh, we're so in love," she gushes. "Seriously, Viktor legit passed out when we found out I was pregnant the first time, but he's such a good dad, like he was born for it. He's over the moon at getting to do it all over again with this one." She starts rubbing circles over the baby bump she's sporting. "By Thanksgiving we'll be a family of four."

"That's awesome. You know, I keep hearing all about how I'm not supposed to drink the water around here."

Ella snorts. "I would say that's good advice."

Scarlett makes a *bah* sound. "Evan and Holly were first. She was in my job, new to her career, super focused and awesome in the role. And he was relentless, but he had a bit of a reputation as a ladies' man and the team has a non-fraternization policy. But it all worked out for them. They have three kids now, which makes my head spin just to think about it."

"Then it was Georg and Pam," Ella adds.

"Yes, Pam came here to work in physical therapy and Georg was a hot mess, but they managed to figure it all out, and now they're adopting Tyler's two siblings."

"And then you guys," Ella says.

"And then Vik and me," Scarlett confirms with a little *ta-da* wave of the hands.

"And none of you got fired for violating the non-fraternization policy, huh?"

Scarlett backs away as the photographer starts giving me instructions on how to pose and smile for shots. She scrutinizes the first few shots, then answers, "Well, Max Terry is a bit of a softie and he's for whatever makes the players perform at their best. But I think Pam nearly got fired at one point. You'd have to ask her about it, though."

"I'll pass. Probably none of my business."

"Well, just be careful. Cupid's arrow seems to be pretty wickedly accurate around here. Even wild-boy Tyler got felled by it. Biggest player in the group and now he's a man in lurve with Georg's sister, Zoya."

As the photographer continues his work, Scarlett and Ella converse off to the side, Ella suggesting that Scarlett and Viktor try one of Devon's cooking classes one night as a date. Of course, any mention of Devon Pearson catches my attention, though I try to make myself seem focused on my photo shoot.

"Oh, believe me," Scarlett says. "I've tried. He's terrified of anything cooking related, thinks he'll surely burn down the kitchen if he tries. We booked a couple's massage date for next weekend instead. I'm looking forward to it, but I still want something, you know...*epic*."

"Well, I'm thinking about going," another of Scarlett's team says from her perch by the door. "Just to stare at Aiden and Mikhail."

"Tell me about Devon's class?" I ask, unable to stop my curiosity. She mentioned a side gig, but I didn't get the details.

"Oh, Devon's doing a personalized nutrition and cooking class once a week. It's really geared toward athletes, but I think it would work for anyone."

"Well, I got divorced about six months ago and my diet's been pretty lazy." I try to sound casual. "Might be good to figure out how to feed myself something other than frozen dinners."

"Yeah," Scarlett agrees. "Seriously, I'm putting you on the bachelor hot list. Can't have you turning into Fat Thor. You should totally go. Devon's awesome."

She's more than awesome.

I know I can't be with Devon openly right now, but maybe going to her classes would give me a chance to be near her and to support her business. The more successful she is, the sooner she can launch. Not that I want to lose a good employee, but having her not working for the Crush makes being with her more of a possibility. Is that manipulative on my part? Probably.

Is it a way to see her without everyone thinking it's weird? Absolutely.

"It'd be a good way for you to meet people in your new city," Ella adds. Her face scrunches up. "But don't meet anyone special too soon. We need to market you as a hot bachelor, ride that sexy single train for a hot minute."

Too late. Already met someone special.

"I am not a piece of meat, ladies."

Everyone laughs. and Scarlett says, "Bud didn't do fun things. It'll be so nice having a GM who does fun things with us. You're younger and hipper, and I think you'll provide a real boost for the staff. A few of them pop into Devon's classes, and I think it would go a long way for you to show up and be, you know, human with them."

"I keep hearing about this plateau everyone thinks the team has hit," I say as I get manhandled by the photographer, who puts me in position and tells me to give him a serious look.

"It's not, like a plateau." Scarlett takes a photo with her phone and explains, "For Instagram, a little preview."

"The front line is in great shape, really connected," Ella says. "I think everyone's just holding their breath, waiting for the bubble to burst, you know? Like someone gets injured or takes an early retirement or whatever, and then the magic is broken."

I can't stop thinking about what Ella said for the rest of the day.

Being the GM of a team at the top of its game? Trying to keep it there at the top, avoiding the eventual fall from grace for as long as possible? It's a ton of pressure.

I have to keep my head in the game here. Vegas is the big leagues, and the stakes are brutally high. I need to keep the Crush at the top, and I can't do that if I'm distracted by sneaking around with one of my employees.

I hate even thinking of Devon in that way. She's so much more than one of my employees. Still, the situation's not sitting right. It's not ideal for her, either. I'll have to think on this. I want to support her, to show her we can be friendly and professional while we still work together.

I know it would be best for me to just stay away from Devon Pearson altogether. Problem is, I don't think I can.

I've developed a full-blown addiction.

20
sexy salmon sensation

Devon

What started as a small group, maybe five or six, has now tripled in size. My small cooking class has grown immensely, thanks mostly to word of mouth from my initial guinea pigs.

I do have a private client now, too, a couple who compete in triathlons together. They're both attorneys here in Vegas, and when they're not working (which is most of the time), they're training, which means they have little time to manage their nutrition.

Evan and his wife, Holly, are here. They've taken the workspace right up front. Holly says, "We got a babysitter. This is date night for us."

Her husband, team captain for the Crush, gives me a lopsided grin. "Holly is back on strict nutrition now that we're done having babies. No more donut holes and Funyuns."

"Ew. Evan, when have you ever seen me eat a Funyun?" Holly asks with a laugh.

"Only the three times I got you pregnant, babe. Of which I am fully to blame." He kisses her on the cheek and winks at me.

"You landed yourself a real winner there, Holly."

"Don't I know it," she says with a look of pure love at her handsome husband.

"Are you still running a lot?"

She nods. "I have a double running stroller, which makes for a much more challenging run, but since we have three now, I have to have someone to watch the other one while I go."

"I tried to convince her to wear him in a backpack but that was a no-go," Evan jokes. "But seriously, look at these guns. Running with two is like a full-body workout."

He pushes Holly's arm up and has her make a muscle, even though she rolls her eyes and laughs about it. Holly's always been in great shape. She doesn't look like she's lost a single day between those babies. It's amazing how she manages being a parent and owning her own business. She and Evan make it look easy.

Looking around the room, my heart swells to see so many of my coworkers here to support my new business. Not just them but others who have heard about this through the grapevine and made it a priority to come check things out. I'm really starting to think I can make this thing a reality.

Everyone's talking, bantering, and getting to know each other, so I bang a wooden spoon on the counter in front of me to get their attention. It's a bigger group, so I don't want to waste time. Just as I'm about to open my mouth and welcome everyone, the door opens at the back, and a tall guy with his head down steps through. But when he looks up, I freeze mid-step. Grant Gerard just walked in through the door to my cooking class.

Wait just a little minute here. Grant Gerard just walked in through the door to my cooking class?

The fact he's in attendance aside, the man really is something to look at. He's not wearing a suit, which he rocks like nobody's business, but in dark jeans and a Crush quarter-zip. He looks just as delicious in casual clothes as he does…well, any other way.

I think I like him naked the best.

I give my head a little shake to clear away the naughty thoughts. Necessary so I can even remotely hope to teach this class coherently. But still, my toes curl as he strides confidently to an empty seat near the front and plops down. A cheeky lopsided grin from him and I'm nearly set on fire. I clearly feel the heat rising in my cheeks as our eyes meet. Trying to nod casually in introduction, I probably look more like I'm having a seizure.

Pull it together, Pearson.

I'm supposed to be a professional, yet here I am, blushing like a schoolgirl in front of a roomful of people because Grant Gerard just came in and smiled at me.

"Thanks for coming, everyone." Somehow, I manage to speak, forcing my focus back onto the rest of the class. "I'm overwhelmed to see so many of you here tonight. Because of the size of the class, it'll be hard to do something totally individualized. However, I'll come around to each station while we work and show you how some basic substitutions and additions can help you maximize your nutritional goals."

"What are we making tonight, chef?" Gia yells from the back, where she shares a station with her new boy-toy Mikhail. His dark hair is wild on top of his head tonight. He looks like he might have just rolled out of bed, and the way his dark eyes glint when he looks at Gia, I bet I can guess just whose bed he visited prior to class.

"Since we have a few couples here tonight on date night, I thought we'd make what I'm calling Sexy Salmon Sensation." I feel my cheeks go even hotter as the weight of Grant's stare falls on me. I take a deep breath to steady myself before adding, "Healthy food can taste great and also be sexy. Even the making of a great meal can be sexy. So this will be fun."

I manage to keep it together while walking everyone through the ingredients and the cooking plan. As I lead folks through the steps, I take a few breaks to check in with my clients who have specific nutritional needs. Some need extra calories, and some want higher protein. That's what I love about nutrition instruction though. It's not hard to modify the most basic meal to ensure nutrition needs are met. We talk about substitutes and add-ons, but I save my check-in with Grant until I've seen everyone else first.

"Welcome, Mr. Gerard," I say as I make my way to his workstation. He's the only one without a partner, which I feel badly about. "I wasn't expecting you."

"I'm sorry," he says as he flips on the gas cooktop. "I signed up like ten minutes before class. After I'd hemmed and hawed about whether I should sign up at all for another ten minutes before that."

"Well, no reason to fret about it. You're always welcome here."

"I just wanted to support your new business," he says. "And maybe meet some people, I guess?"

"Well, this *is* a fun group." I try to sound neutral and light even though he makes me want to do all manner of forbidden, naked things.

Making some lame gesture about how he needs a partner, I end up staying at Grant's station and walking the group through each step of the recipe from there. Grant's intensity is at level-ten, and I'm pretty sure I'm the focus rather than the recipe I chose for tonight. How is it possible for him to both rattle me and arouse me at the same time?

I have to step away occasionally to check on the

other students, but each time I return to his station, I start breathing like I haven't breathed in days. *What is this physical thing he does to me?*

I share thoughts on plating and presentation once we get through the preparation. "Gotta make sure it looks sexy," I say, grinning and trying not to look over at Grant. "Once you have it plated, please enjoy the fruits of our labor and eat up."

After making the rounds and taking photos of everyone with their plated meals, I grab a stool at Grant's workspace and share the plate he's prepared. From the back of the room, I hear Mikhail ask, "What did I do wrong?"

His face is twisted in distaste, his fork held midair, and his lips pursed. Gia is laughing so hard she's crying, bent over, clutching her stomach.

At the next workstation over Aiden, accompanied by one of the showgirls, Anna, who has been at each and every one of my classes, is also laughing. Mikhail looks at him helplessly as Aiden says, "I may have put waaaayyy too much salt on that. And, like, five other spices the recipe didn't call for."

"Aw, dude," Mikhail says. "Why did you sabotage my sexy salmon? That's messed *up*."

"Payback for the rookie prank you pulled on me earlier this week."

Gia, still laughing, says, "Come on, Mikhail, you can share mine."

"Oh, goodie," Aiden says. "Going home alone

again." He starts to sing "All By Myself" loudly and very much off-key, much to everyone's amusement.

"I didn't know you two were roomies," Evan says.

"Just while I look for a place of my own," Aiden says. "I haven't decided where I want to be."

"Well, I'd be careful, then," Evan says, grinning. "You might find a spider in your bed or some cheese whizz in your hand one night. Mikhail does *not* let a prank go unanswered."

Mikhail just smiles innocently in response. Grant's right about Crush team members. They are like a family. And despite the proverbial line I've kept between myself and my coworkers, I'll miss this atmosphere when I'm working on my own.

After we all clean up, folks thank me and start to trickle out. I use their exit as a chance to escape to the supply closet, arms laden with spice bottles. I take a few deep breaths, trying to steady myself. I've been hot and bothered all night, with Grant constantly watching me. I have to stay professional around him. Especially in situations like these, where there are Crush players and staff around. But damn, why does he have to be so friggin' hot? I mean, seriously? I haven't been this attracted to a man since, well, ever. Maybe my ex, but I was a different person then, just a young college student blinded by talent and hubris.

Still, the thought of my ex douses the heat a little, enough that I can stand up straight and take a calming breath. But as soon as I get myself under control, I turn, and there he is, looming in the doorway.

"I enjoyed the class," he says, the sound of his deep voice rumbling straight to all the tingly places. "You're really amazing at this. At being a coach and a teacher. And it's clear you love it."

Mouth hanging open, I suck in a breath and turn away. I can't fall under this spell. "Thanks," I manage, before letting the breath back out as I fuss with the arrangement of the spice rack.

I hear him take a step forward, his footstep soft on the tile floor. Closing my eyes, I try not to think about how close he is, how small the space is, how easy it would be to...

His lips are at my ear when he whispers, "I can't stop thinking about you. I've tried all week, but I just can't seem to stay away."

The feeling of his breath on my ear, his intoxicating scent, his nearness, it sets me on fire. My nipples go hard beneath the lace of my bra. I can't look at him, though. It will make it worse. Still, I allow myself to whisper, "I feel the same."

A hand at my waist, and I nearly fall back against the solidness of him.

"You know we can't be seen together, though. Grant, please."

"I know," he says, his lips still grazing my ear. His free hand slips around me to the hem of my skirt, pushing it up, fingers playing at the skin of my thigh, then higher. Fingertips play at the overheated space between my legs, my panties soaked. There's no denying how I feel.

Lips and teeth along my ear, my neck, my jaw. Fingers pushing aside thin cloth to find my folds, to slip inside. Fingering me, kissing me, I'm helpless to do anything but hold on to the shelves on either side of me. "That's it, beautiful girl. Ride my fingers." *Oh God, his voice.* "Your pussy is the hottest fuckin' thing. Tastes like heaven. I wish I was on my knees right now." He kisses my neck and I shudder. "You deserve to be fucking worshipped. By *me*." My heart is beating erratically now. I am so turned on. More kisses rain down the side of my neck as his fingers move wickedly inside me. "Can you feel how hard I am for you right now? How much I wish it was my cock inside you making you come." *Oh God. I want that. I want that so much. Him. I want him.* "I can hear how turned on you are, Devon. You're fucking incredible."

All those dirty words coming out of his mouth. His cock pressing into me. His fingers. His hot breath and ridiculous kisses. Riding the wave of pleasure as I go up and up and up toward climax. *And then I'm there. Fuck, am I there.*

When I come, I practically bite my own tongue to keep from crying out. It goes on and on, reality slipping away as I get lost in the pleasure he's making me feel.

From the classroom space, I hear someone say my

name, and Grant must too, because he quickly pulls away. I'm left confused for a moment, still spaced out by the amazing orgasm I've just had. I smooth over my ponytail and pull my skirt to rights as Grant watches, wicked smirk and all. "That was fun," he says.

"Someone's looking for me. Can you go out and let them know I'm in the restroom?"

Another lopsided grin and he's out the door. Me? I put my head on the cool metal of the shelving unit, trying to make sense of what just happened.

When I finally make it back out to the classroom, Gia gives me a knowing look before saying, "That was delicious, chef. Too bad we didn't have time for *dessert.*"

I frown. "This is a healthy cooking class."

She grins. "But dessert is so much fun. Oh...what's the word I'm looking for? Naughty?"

Mikhail asks if she's ready to go, so I don't need to come up with a retort—thankfully, since I'm still brain-dead from whatever spell Grant just put on me. They wave and head out, leaving me alone with Grant. He stares at me for an extra-long second before shoving his hands in his pockets.

"I'm gonna text you my address," he says deliberately. "Just...for what it's worth. Thanks for the great class."

He strides out, and I hear him say good night to someone just before Holly pops back in.

"Oh, hey," I say, surprised to see her. "I thought you guys were long gone."

Holly walks to her workstation and grabs her purse from underneath. "Can't leave without my Mary Poppins bag."

"Yep, wouldn't be good to leave it here, that's for sure. Evan still outside?"

"He went to get the car," she says, before pushing her lips into a weird little pout thing. "You know, I found it interesting that you disappeared and then Grant disappeared..."

Shame swells in my stomach as I busy myself by sweeping the floor. "I just ran to put the spices away. He must have gone to the restroom."

"Mm-hmm," she hums. "He came out sporting a semi. Just sayin'."

"I don't...I don't know what you're talking about." I'm a terrible liar. Like, really bad. So, I don't usually do it. But I'm doing it now with Holly. And it's so obvious I want to crawl into a hole and die.

Holly's smile looks more like a grimace as she dances back and forth from one foot to the other. "Look, Devon, I'm not judging. I'm not. Look at how Evan and I snuck around. And I tried turning him away. And I tried acting like I didn't like him. And you know what? I did like him. And you like who you like."

"But," I say quietly.

"But," she repeats, "he's the GM here, brand new,

and the boss of pretty much everyone, including you. He can't start his career here with a reputation for sleeping with his staff."

"We're not...doing that." It's limp as it comes out of my mouth. Another lie. I feel sick. I meet Holly's knowing gaze and she looks sympathetic.

"I've known you for a few years now and I've never taken you for a liar," she says gently. "You're my friend and I care about you. I want you to be happy. And I know you get a lot of male attention and, quite frankly, you're mostly oblivious to it. So he must be something pretty special to get your attention. Even more so to be worth sneaking around when there's so much on the line. But please be careful."

There's little I can say right now that would make this better. "We met before he got the job," I whisper. "We didn't know."

She nods. "I get it. But things are what they are and let's be real, it's not going to be him who loses his job if word gets around."

"I know. You're right." I take a shaky breath. "Thank you. For caring. I'm really embarrassed."

Holly steps over to give me a hug. She really does know how this feels. And it worked out for them, so I have a tiny moment of hope that maybe it could work for Grant and me, too. I know, though, that it's different. Evan was a player, and she was staff. He wasn't her boss or her boss's boss. And that's the difference.

"No need to be embarrassed," she says as we pull apart. "He's hot, and you two make a lot of sense actually. Just be careful. Also, this was awesome tonight. Just what we two old, married people needed. I'm going to see if my husband wants to park and make out before we head home."

This gets a laugh out of me. "Well, good luck with that."

Holly winks and heads out the door.

Alone in the classroom, I find a stool and sit, my thoughts on this situation with Grant. I really like him. I can't and won't lie about it. He's sexy and kind and smart and accomplished. And he's totally forbidden and off-limits. He has to be. *"But things are what they are and let's be real, it's not going to be him who loses his job if word gets around."* Holly is right. I've thought a lot about Grant's career, but I shouldn't neglect my own. Four years ago, this job was my absolute saving grace. I am good at what I do, and even if my plans to stay with the Crush are already on a countdown, I don't want to start a new career with a negative.

Toying with my phone, I pull up his text. His address is there, an open invitation. But I know I shouldn't go. We should cool it for now, at least while I still work for the Crush. My business is going well, but who knows if it's going to stay steady. I'm not ready to just quit my job yet. The thought of cutting the cord like that is too scary.

I need to talk to him, to tell him that I really like him but that this has to stop. He can't just show up at my classes. He can't be finding me in the supply closet and using his magical fingers to get me off like that.

Even if my vagina hates me for thinking it.

We can't do the things we keep doing.

I will seriously miss his magical penis.

I'm going to go tell him. Right now. This ends tonight. *For now...*

21
why christmas?

Grant

When I hear the knock at my door, I know it's her.

My place is a little way out of town, a standalone condo in a newer development. I wanted something quiet, out from the city. Somewhere allowing some separation between my job and the team to my personal space.

I fling the door open wide, and there she is, toned arms exposed by the thin, blue sleeveless blouse she's wearing. Her legs are long, so long in her gray pencil skirt and black high heels. Her hair hangs long and sleek down her back in a ponytail. I've just looked at her for two hours in the kitchen, but the sight of her now feels new again. I've had the scent of her on my fingers for the last thirty minutes, and it took a great deal of restraint not to get myself off with her taste on my tongue. The sounds of her as she came on my hand in that supply closet. Her quiet moans. *I can't get enough of this woman.*

She's so gorgeous she literally takes my breath away.

"I, um, need a drink after looking at you."

"I make you…thirsty?"

"In only the best way. Come in?"

She doesn't step forward right away. In fact, she frowns a little and shifts her weight, planting herself just outside the threshold.

"I feel just the same as you do, Grant," she says after a moment. "But people noticed today. Not everyone, I don't think, but a few. Gia noticed…"

"But Gia already knows," I argue.

"But Mikhail?"

"He's oblivious. No way. The only way he'd figure it out is if your friend told him."

"She wouldn't. But Holly noticed, too. It's too dangerous, Grant. This is a new job for you. A good one with a great team. And they need your brain and your energy and your creativity. I don't want you to jeopardize that. And I'm not ready to give up my job yet, either. Soon, but not yet. We have to stop this. We have to, for both of our careers."

I can see what she's trying to do here. She's a good person. She doesn't want me to get in trouble or to get a reputation. And she's a rule follower. She's a careful person, and this is a big risk for her. And I agree with her. But—

"I just don't think I can stay away from you, Devon. I don't want to." It's more an admission of defeat than anything else.

"And I don't want you to," she says quickly. "I don't. But we *have* to, don't you see that?"

"There's some kind of magic between us, Devon. You feel it. I feel it. And I feel like we both know better than to just throw it away."

Devon's shoulders, held high as she mustered the resolve to tell me we needed to keep our distance, slump now. She lets out a weary breath and shakes her head. "Please don't make this harder than it is. Grant, we have to keep our distance. Not forever. Just until I get my business launched and am able to quit my job with the team. Let's give it some space, show some restraint. And that means no coming to my class. It's too much of a temptation to be around you."

"I came to class because I wanted to see you, but also to learn about you. And I wasn't lying when I said it was a good opportunity for me to be sociable and meet people. I enjoyed being there tonight."

"Grant." Devon rolls her head back and groans. "You are not making this any easier."

"I'm not trying to make it easy on you, beautiful." I step forward.

Devon starts to say something, but I don't hear it. I don't want to hear it, quite frankly, so I silence her with a kiss. It's rough, a little desperate. She stiffens at first, and I wonder if I've made a mistake. But when she gives in, it's like ice thawing under the winter sunshine. She sighs against my mouth, opening for me, letting me kiss her how I want.

And I want.

I pull her inside, kicking the door closed, leading her to the bedroom. Her sexy heels go first, then the skirt. The blouse follows, leaving her in only her creamy lace bra and panties. It only takes me a moment to pull my T-shirt over my head and my jeans down over my hips. I'm single-minded, crazed for her, already hard beneath my boxer shorts.

Taking her face in my hands, I kiss her again, long and sensuous, as her body's curves fit against mine. Her hand slips beneath my shorts to take hold of my cock. She strokes, and I could come just from her touch, just from the feel of her supple lips on mine. When she gracefully moves to her knees and pulls the cloth down over my hips, I could die. Just the sight of this beautiful woman on her knees, ready to please me, is enough.

When her amazing lips encircle my cock, I can't look away. It's mesmerizing, watching her take all of me, sliding her lips back and forth along the full length of me. It doesn't take long before I'm ready to come in her mouth, but I don't. Instead, I back away, holding out a hand to help her to her feet.

"You're going to be the end of me," I growl,

tugging her against me, planting a hard kiss on her lips.

"You'd deserve every bit of it, too," she answers, the ghost of a smile playing at the corners of her mouth.

In between kisses, I ask in a low murmur, "Did you like what I did to you earlier? Fucking you with my fingers until you came?"

She moans in the affirmative, her legs stretching open as I push her back against the bed. She sits, looking up at me with her sexy eyes, hair coming loose from her formerly sleek ponytail. She's rumpled and needy and really fucking gorgeous, waiting on me to join her.

"Do you want more?" I ask, fingers tracing the silk between her legs, feeling the wetness there once more. I'm so hard, I could explode. I want to be inside of her.

She nods and leans back, elbows barely propping her up, legs dangling over the edge of the bed as I pull her panties from her slim hips and down her long legs. They drop to the floor, a mere scrap of silky fabric I'm irrationally jealous of.

I can't help myself from putting my tongue to her swollen clit as I push two fingers inside, so very wet and warm and pulsing around them.

Devon's moans are nearly too much for me to handle. And when she unclasps her bra and unleashes those perfect tits for me, I could die a happy man. I suck on one dusky brown nipple at a time, still fucking her with my fingers.

"I want you inside of me," she breathes. "Please."

Reluctantly, I step away, just long enough to grab a condom from the nightstand. When I turn back, she's touching herself, one hand working her clit, the other pinching a nipple.

"I could watch you do that all day." My voice sounds gravelly and thick, even to my ears.

"But I'd rather you do it for me. Come here." She crooks a finger naughtily at me.

No further invitation needed.

"I want to see your perfect ass when I fuck you this time." I help her up and turn her around. Bent over the bed, she's a goddess, legs parted, hair trailing down her back. Devon is a woman who takes very good care of her body and it shows in her lightly muscular frame. When she turns her head, and I see her bite down on her bottom lip, it's very nearly my undoing.

She gasps when I touch the tip of my cock to her sex, sliding up and down the folds, pressing on her clit, teasing her. When she pushes her ass toward me, I can't wait another second to take her.

I slide in deep, burying my cock to the root, grunting out the question, "How do you want it?" but not waiting for an answer before beginning to move in long, measured strokes.

"Hard. Fast." She braces her arms in preparation

for what's to come, readying herself for one wild fuck I fully intend to deliver.

"Your wish is my command."

Harder and faster is what I give her.

We both get lost somewhere in the frenzy. It doesn't take long before sweat starts to bead on my forehead, my cock growing harder with every penetration into her depths, and with every sexy moan floating out of her mouth.

"Come for me, beautiful Devon. Come *with* me."

She answers me with an orgasm.

It's only when her cunt clamps down around my cock do I let myself go.

Climaxing with a roar, I spill every last drop out of me and into her.

WE'RE STILL COLLAPSED TOGETHER, folded over the edge of my bed, breathing heavily, trying to recover from whatever wild fantasy fucking that just was.

Only the best single sexual experience of my life.

"You okay after all that?" I ask against her ear, unable to resist kissing my way up her neck, and then across her jaw, and finally to find her lips where her cheek rests on the bed. The need to be close and connected to her still strong.

"Mmm, oh yeah," she purrs back at me. Both of us

seem to be relishing the heady afterglow of some really spectacular sex, just breathing and sharing the moment.

At some point, I reluctantly move off her and head to the en suite, where I turn on the shower.

Waiting for the water to heat, I think about why it's so easy being with Devon. Is it only because she's this amazing, beautiful, sensual woman? Or is it something more beyond that? Am I starting to fall for her? Or has that already happened?

All questions for another time, I suppose, as she's joined me in the en suite, looking almost otherworldly with her hair streaming down over her shoulders, standing naked in the doorway. I take a mental image of how she looks in the moment because I want to remember this.

In silence, she steps into the shower and under the hot water, taking my hand and pulling me in behind her.

My arms go around her, and we stand together under the hot spray raining down over our bodies. We wash each other, kissing and fondling. She's so responsive to my touching her, I make her come once more while washing between her legs.

When we're finished, and I wrap her in an oversized towel, she lays her head on my chest and closes her eyes. So I pick her up and take her back to my bed, where we crawl naked under the covers. I pull her into my arms and hold her, wishing our time together didn't have to expire at midnight like in a fairy tale.

"I like you a lot, Devon Pearson." I kiss her forehead.

"I like you, too, Grant Gerard." Her words are followed by a yawn. "Too much, it appears."

"Never too much."

She's quiet for a long time before finally saying, "I just want you to be successful here. The rumor mill is crazy and if word got out…"

"It won't," I say, but I know I can't make that promise. I don't know this place, these people. Devon said Evan's wife already said something. I know their story is similar, a player and a staff member. I know Max Terry blessed off on three internal relationships already. Perhaps he'd make an exception for Devon and me as well?

"This has to be the last time, Grant. At least until I can set out on my own."

I think of a million things, a million ways to respond, but nothing comes out. I've never been a liar and I won't start now. I won't tell her that I'll stay away because I don't think I can. And I know I don't want to. So, instead of answering, I ask, "What's your favorite holiday?"

She gives me a sleepy half-smile. "Christmas."

"Are you spiritual?"

"I guess? I grew up going to church and I guess I have some sense of a higher power, but I could be better about it. My grandmother would roll over in her grave though. She raised my older brother and me after our parents died in a boating accident when I was fifteen. He was eighteen and just about to leave for college. I haven't been to church since *I* left home for college."

"Oh wow. That must have been really hard for you at such a young age, losing both of your parents. I'm so sorry, Devon. You've been through a lot."

"Yeah. I miss them but it was a long time ago and my brother and I were left well supported financially, and we had our grandma who loved us to distraction. Losing her five years ago hit me much harder, honestly. I'd just gotten divorced and then I lost my grandma Josephine at the end of that same year, and that really sucked. So I pulled up stakes in Florida and moved to Las Vegas, made a fresh start with my life. I took the job here and haven't looked back since, really. This is my home now."

"And your brother?"

"Brett works in international finance and travels all over the globe for his job. We don't see each other that much, but we talk all the time. He comes once or twice a year to Vegas, usually on business, so we spend time together then. I have some aunts and uncles and cousins in Florida who come to Vegas for vacations sometimes, but that's about it for family."

"Then why Christmas?"

She sighs and closes her eyes. "I don't know. It just

feels warm, I guess. Something about the decorations and the twinkling lights and the idea of giving someone something that's perfect for them? And I like to bake. It's like the longest cheat week of the year."

I can't help but chuckle. "Fair enough. I'm a Halloween fan."

"Halloween? I don't see that, somehow."

"Oh, yeah. Total cosplay nerd."

"No way." Devon opens one eye, eyebrows knitted, expression dubious.

"Yeah, I'm totally kidding. I like Christmas best, too. My dad is one of those neighbors who goes overkill with the Christmas lights. I can't tell you how many hours I spent on the roof hanging lights with him as a kid. I learned a few things over the years. The cookies are a pretty awesome perk of the season as well. In a few months, I'm very much looking forward to tasting your Christmas cookies, Chef Pearson." I wiggle my eyebrows at her salaciously.

"Deal," she says with a laugh that turns into another yawn, her pretty, brown eyes fluttering closed one last time as she drifts off to sleep.

I spend a long time just looking at her, stroking her hair, tracing the curve of her jaw with my fingertips.

I want so badly to tell her I haven't felt like this in a very long time, that I'm so glad we happened to be at the same hotel that night after my interview. How I'm so grateful for being blindsided at seeing her in her office on my first day here. It feels like it can't all just be a coincidence. It feels like maybe we were meant to find each other here in Las Vegas. *I know full well I'm falling for her.*

As my own eyes get heavy, I hold her tighter, also knowing full well, it might be the last time I get to for a while.

22

therapist uber drivers

Devon

The sun is warm on my face as I come back from a deep, deep sleep. At first, I'm confused by my surroundings, but when I feel the weight of an arm draped over my midsection, I remember.

I spent the night with Grant Gerard, and I remember exactly *how* we spent our night together, too.

Yes, I came here to tell him we needed to stay away, and I ended up spending the night. Zero willpower when it comes to this man. Zero!

He's dead asleep still, on his stomach, face turned toward me with his arm stretched out across me. His usually perfect, thick hair is wild on his head, and a five o'clock shadow gives him a sexy, rugged look.

I slip away, my feet hitting the soft carpeting as I stretch toward the ceiling, my body hurting in all the good ways. Grant doesn't stir, so I take a moment to memorize him. His lips, his nose, his jawline. And his back. Good lord, his back. The back of Grant is all sculpted muscles in a broad-shouldered package tapering down to a V that's even more carved on the front of him than his ass is on the backside of him.

Male back perfection.

Can a man have a sexy back?

If his name is Grant Gerard, then yes, he can have a sexy everything.

Frankly, there's not much about Grant that doesn't turn me on. His body is a well-oiled machine, for sure, and he's a pro in bed, but it's more than just his physical beauty. I do really like him. I connect with him. I can talk to him, and I feel like he really sees me, wants to know me. I'm not just a pretty face to him, like I seem to be for a lot of men. I haven't had such a genuine and comfortable connection with a man in a long, long time. Maybe ever, honestly, because the connections we make with people when we're barely more than children, how real can those really be? I mean, we hardly know ourselves at that age. We change so much. But now, as an adult with a career? This is what I didn't know I was missing.

Which is why it hurts so much, knowing that this must definitely be the last time we're together.

It really is the cruelest twist of fate that he's my boss's boss. The non-fraternization policy at the Crush is a running joke at this point, considering three staff members have now married players. But this is different. It's different because we're both staff, and there's a power dynamic that can't be ignored. Having a relationship with a staff member would be viewed as inappropriate, casting a strange light on him in a brand-new role. I've heard such positive things about his energy, commitment, and drive as GM, and the Crush will only benefit from that. I'd hate to hear people say he's a womanizer, which is probably how it would be perceived. *Even though, I know he's anything but.*

I can't help but think back to that first night and how awed he'd seemed that I'd said yes to a drink with him. He's far more humble than you'd expect from such an incredible sportsman. But the naysayers wouldn't care to hear the part about how we met before he was even hired. People tune out those details they don't want to know. *He deserves better than that.* And I do too.

I'm teary as I gather my clothing and dress as quietly as possible. I really don't want him to wake up. I don't want to have this conversation with Grant yet again.

It makes me so anxious I fear I might throw up, quite honestly.

In his kitchen, I find a piece of paper and a pen, and write a note.

GRANT,

THIS HAS TO BE THE LAST TIME. I THINK YOU KNOW ALREADY HOW MUCH I REALLY DO LIKE YOU, BUT WE HAVE TO KEEP THINGS PROFESSIONAL. I'LL DO MY JOB AND YOU'LL DO YOURS AND WE'LL STAY OUT OF EACH OTHER'S ORBIT FROM NOW ON. I DON'T WANT TO BE THE RUIN OF THIS PROFESSIONAL OPPORTUNITY FOR YOU, NOR AM I READY TO GIVE UP MY JOB JUST YET. PLEASE STAY AWAY. PLEASE DON'T COME TO MY CLASSES ANYMORE. YOU KNOW THIS IS THE RIGHT THING FOR US. I ONLY WANT THE BEST FOR YOU IN YOUR NEW POSITION, AS I KNOW YOU WANT THE SAME FOR ME.

WHEN THE TIME IS RIGHT FOR US TO BE TOGETHER AGAIN, WE'LL KNOW, BUT THAT TIME CANNOT BE NOW.

BE WELL,
DEVON

I TOOK a cab to Grant's place last night because I didn't want to risk anyone seeing my car, knowing I was spending the night with him.

Good decision on my part because I'd be totally incapacitated for driving myself right now because of the tears. Maybe tears is not the right descriptor. It's more like big, ugly crying. Sobbing that has my Uber driver looking very concerned for me.

"I've had a breakup," I offer, which isn't the total truth, but it's also not a lie.

"Any guy who would break up with a woman as beautiful as you is an idiot."

"That's sweet, but it was I who did the breaking up. It was my choice."

"You don't seem happy about it. Or relieved, or whatever other things people feel when they do the breaking up. I wouldn't know. I have been married for thirty years."

"I'm not happy or relieved." I shake my head. "It's just the best thing for both of us right now."

"Sometimes, we think things are best for us, but really they are not."

"It can be hard to tell sometimes," I agree, suddenly overcome by nausea. "Hey, I'm feeling a bit car sick. Could you roll down the windows?"

He obliges as I put all my focus on not throwing up. Thankfully, it's not a long ride, but by the time he drops me at my building, and I take the elevator up to my floor, I'm pretty sure I'm going to puke. I barely get to the bathroom before I lose everything in my stomach, and violently. *I cannot recall a time that I've felt so stressed that I'm this ill.*

Once I'm pretty sure I can stand upright again, I turn on the shower, letting it heat up as I brush my teeth. I look like garbage, with crazy bedhead and dark circles under my swollen eyes. Ugh. *And to think the driver thought this was beautiful.*

The hot water feels amazing, but as I wash myself, I realize how heavy and tender my breasts are. God, this accounts for the sobbing, then. I must be ready to start my period. Well, thank goodness it didn't happen at Grant's. Talk about adding insult to injury. *Hey, let's not see each other anymore. Oh, by the way, I bled on your sheets.* Yikes.

I step out of the shower and pull open my Cycles app on my phone to double-check. Everything's been so hectic, I haven't been paying attention at all—

Oh.

I'm weeks late.

I wrap myself in a towel and sit down on the toilet, staring at my phone as if the dates are magically going to rearrange themselves, back to my normal cycle, which is always like clockwork.

My mind races. Grant and I have had sex, what, three times now? Well, on three occasions? We've used condoms each time—

Oh. Shit.

That first night. He said the condom broke. I'd put it out of my head. *He and his ex-wife tried for years.* Was he lying about that to cover his ass? No. Surely not. I don't know him that well, but I'm pretty certain he's not a liar.

Oh God. The nausea and vomiting. The fatigue and volatile emotions and the low energy.

I don't think this is a virus.

Fuck.

The sickness I feel mixes with anxiety. My head swims, and my mind races. I can hardly remember to breathe as my vision goes blurry. I breathe in and out, in and out, until I can get it together enough to call Gia.

"Good morning," she answers cheerfully.

"Um...I need you to c-come. I think—I nee—I—can you bring me a pregnancy test?"

The line is quiet for a long moment, and then, "I'll be there in fifteen."

And she is. When she lets herself in, she finds me in the same position, wet and towel-clad, sitting on the toilet lid, trying not to pass out from the panic I feel.

"Hey," she says. "So..."

"I'm weeks late." I shove my phone at her. "I'm never late."

"Okay, but you've also been burning the midnight oil on your side gig, plus your day job. Maybe it's just stress."

"And throwing up. So much throwing up. Always in the morning. Gia, I think I actually am pregnant and I am trying really hard not to freak out, but I am. Freaking out."

"Well, let's do the test and be sure, okay? And then

we'll figure out what to do next, depending on the results."

I nod, tears flowing again. She pulls the test out of the box and reads the directions. "Pee on this and then wait three minutes."

In the longest three minutes of my life, I manage to pull on a T-shirt and shorts and to braid my wet hair. When the timer on Gia's phone goes off, we both scramble to look at the test, where two side-by-side lines appear.

"Two lines?" I ask weakly.

"Pregnant."

23
well-oiled machines take fewer risks

Grant

The players are all back from their summer engagements, so I've called a players' meeting in order to introduce myself to the team as a whole. Many of our guys teach summer hockey or play in summer leagues overseas, and they all tend to come back about three weeks before training camp starts.

I've met a few of them over the summer, particularly the rookies and the first-string, but this is the first I'm seeing them all in one place.

"Good morning, gentlemen," I say as the guys settle in. "I'm Grant Gerard, now GM, for this fine organization. I've met a bunch of you in different settings, but it's nice to see you all in one place."

"Didn't you play for Canada in Sochi?" I hear from the back of the crowd.

"I did, and you are?"

"Cal," he says, arms folded over his chest as he leans casually against a row of lockers. "Goalie."

"Nice to meet you, Cal. And also, from what I've heard, resident collegiate scholar for the Crush."

"Meh," he answers with a one-shouldered shrug.

The rest of the team laughs, and Tyler Lockhardt chimes in, "The Professor is *meh* about most things other than hockey and his rock star fiancée."

"Well, as long as he's not *meh* about hockey," I say to another round of chuckles. "Which is a good segue, actually. I've had the chance to settle into the job now, and it's been a pleasure to learn about this team and its culture. The staff in the administrative offices have been amazing, and I feel really good about the training and therapy staff. There have been a couple of areas of concern, though, and as a result, I've decided—with Max Terry's blessing—to make some changes on the game side of the house."

There's rumbling as the guys look around the room, trying to figure out what changes I've made. I can see their wheels turning. Who's missing?

"I wanted you to hear about all of this from me directly, which is why I brought you all here today. First, Coach Brown is still with us."

An audible sigh of relief. Coach Brown has taken this team to great heights. I'd be insane to cut him loose, but new GMs have done weirder things to make their mark.

"However," I continue, "I have cut loose the

secondary coaching staff. I need a more diverse, scrappier, more innovative team to work with the second-string. Those guys aren't getting enough minutes on the ice, mainly because they're not prepared. We're asking a lot of our first-string. There is no room for an injury because there's no one who can step in and fill their shoes completely. Don't get me wrong, there's talent on the second- and third-string lines, but that talent needs investment. It needs molding and coaching, and I just didn't feel like the investment was there from a group of guys whose job was to make that happen."

There are some mixed reactions among the guys. Some seem to agree with what I'm saying, while others seem a little shell-shocked that I've chosen to release the bulk of our coaching staff. I wait for a second, just to see if there are any comments or questions. When no one speaks up, I move on.

"From a player perspective, we've got some clear superstars. We've invested a lot in big names, big performers, crowd pleasers." I make eye contact with Evan, Georg, Tyler, Boris, and Viktor, who has his huge arms crossed over his even huge-er chest. He's massive—I don't think I quite realized just how big the Mad Russian really was until right now. He was at the very beginning of his career when we played in Sochi.

"Big names put butts in seats," I say. "And the PR team here makes the most of it. I'm super impressed with them, to be honest. Revenue goes up when people love our players. Even more so when our players work well together. And this front line works well together. It's a dream team, a well-oiled machine. It's a line that wins Cups."

"But?" I hear from one of the players. I turn and see that the question comes from Evan, the team captain.

"But well-oiled machines take fewer risks. They can be easy to figure out. People have expectations about their style of play. Now, this isn't news to you, of course, but it needs to be addressed. And that's my job. What if one of you gets seriously injured? What if one of you decides to retire to coaching or management?" I pause for a moment so they're engaged in the question. It's their team, so they should be. "As you know, it messes with the whole dynamic. And while a guy might be good as a fill-in, what's the uptake on getting him to mesh in with what's already in place?"

"I don't know what you're trying to say, but no one gets between me and my bae on the back line," Tyler says, batting his eyelashes at Viktor.

This loosens the tension slightly. Evan, with whom I've had several conversations of late, jumps in. "Guys, this is what we've talked about. And Grant's right, we do need a second- and third-string that can sub in easily and often with as little disruption to our style of play as possible."

"Or that the disruption is innovative enough to

confuse the competition," Cal adds from his post at the back of the room.

"Yes! Yes, that's exactly it. I want a second-string that fits in with the first-string's chemistry. I absolutely want to confuse the opponent and build a bench that the fans care about as much as they care about our stars."

"Sorry, we don't like competition. There's only room for our larger-than-life posters outside the building," Tyler jokes.

"It's a big building," I counter, grinning. "I did make some trades off the second- and third-string lines. The whole list of changes will go out in an email later this week, including who we're picking up. I expect all the contracting to be done in the next day or two. They're good changes, necessary changes, and they've been made with the input of both the team's ownership and the head coach. I'm not making decisions in a vacuum here, and I'm sure as hell not some gunslinger, ready to shoot stuff up around here. But I do have a business to run, and it needs to have a shelf life beyond the individual careers of our top guys."

The players murmur, some of them seeming a little shaken, still. Evan jumps up and stands next to me. He says, "Guys, we needed a shake-up. This is a pivotal season. If we want to be a legacy team, we can't rest on our laurels."

"Well, go on and retire already, you old fart," one

of the guys says in a heavy French Canadian accent. Everyone laughs.

"Maybe I'll take you up on that sometime soon," Evan says, flipping the bird.

We finish up the meeting with a few more questions. As people start to filter out, I grab Evan and ask if he's up for lunch in the pub. As we walk out, I ask who the player was who encouraged his retirement.

"Oh, that's Giroux. He played for me when I was injured and also in the finals last season. He's a bit uptight—it surprises me to see him joke around at all. Though, in hindsight, it may not have been a joke."

Once we're seated and have our lunches ordered, I can't resist asking, "So is retirement really in the cards for you? I've heard all the rumors."

"Nah." He shrugs it off. "I mean, I've thought about it, but I'm still playing well. With three little kids at home, it makes it harder to go on the road. Once Holly and I started, we went whole hog, you know what I mean? Baby, baby, baby, all right in a row. It's a lot for her to manage, along with her own business. I'm sure she'd appreciate it if I switched to a foundation or a management role that kept me on the ground more."

"I get that."

"You played. I heard you had a pretty gruesome injury."

"Yes, forced retirement for me. Tore up my knee

big-time, and right after we won gold in Sochi. I felt like I was at the top of my game with lots of juice left and then, just…poof. Over."

"Damn. That's hard. I'd hate to go out like that."

"It sucked, but I had an aptitude for the business side of things. I miss the play, but I don't miss my body getting wrecked."

"Well, I assure you I'm at one hundred percent, mentally and physically. I'm still committed, and I love this team."

"It's not an inquisition or an interview, Evan. I just wanted to know if there was merit to the rumors. They've been persistent."

"Wishful thinking on the part of some guys not getting enough time or some analysts with too much time on their hands."

"Okay. Well, just let me know if anything changes."

Evan nods as our food comes. He shoves a french fry in his mouth and asks, "So, how are you settling in?"

"Um, good." I take a swig of water to chase the bite of burger I just had. "Thanks. The job's been great. Hard choices to make, but I was hired to do a thing, so I'm doing it."

"Max is a focused owner. He doesn't make shitty choices. I think you're doing a good job, at least from what I can tell. I just, more like, well, I was thinking more, like socially. Are you meeting anyone? Seeing anyone outside the office?"

I stop chewing and stare at him. He's…is he *blushing*? Like he's embarrassed to be asking whatever it is he's trying to ask. And then I remember Devon saying that Evan's wife confronted her after the cooking class I attended. "Look, if you've got something to say, just say it."

"My wife mentioned something about her suspicions. She thought maybe you and Devon Pearson might have had a thing going on. And I'm totally not judging, man. Devon's great, and I sure as hell chased on Holly until she gave in, policy be damned." Evan's shrug is rueful.

A sigh precedes my decision to be honest about the situation. I actually really like Evan. I think we could become friends. "We met before I started. I'd just been offered the job, she was at a conference, and we met in the hotel bar. I figured she was from some other state. We promised not to talk about work or exes. We had a few drinks, talked for a long time. One thing led to another."

"So you thought it was just a one-night stand?"

"I didn't even know her last name, let alone where she worked. And I was pretty fresh off a divorce. But I liked her. I thought about her a lot in the weeks before I moved here. And I was shocked to find out she worked for the Crush."

"I'll bet." Evan chuckles.

"We connect," I say. "I dig her a lot and I think she feels the same, but she's worried about the perception of people thinking I sleep with my staff members. And I get that. She's ended it, anyway, so it doesn't matter much now."

"I'm sorry, man," Evan says sympathetically. "She's probably right, and it's probably for the best, but I get it. So I'm sorry."

"Me, too, man. Me, too."

I spend the rest of the afternoon forcing myself to stay in my office. All that talk about Devon only made me want to walk right down to her office and tell her how stupid this is. Or up to Max's office to ask, no— beg him to let us see each other. Sorta like asking The Godfather for his blessing.

Increasingly distracted as the afternoon wears on, I have to stop myself from reading and rereading her bio on the website like some creeper. How is it possible to miss someone this much when we've only interacted a few times? I'm behaving like some lovestruck teenager.

Honestly, that morning I woke up to find the handwritten note Devon left for me was the worst.

When I walked in on my wife and my friend, that was like a kick to the nuts. I felt sick and angry and betrayed, but deep down, not surprised. It had been over for a long time between Margot and me, but I'd been too blind to notice.

But this thing with Devon? Waking up alone after

another incredible night with her? Finding her note on my kitchen counter? That felt like true loss. A very deep loss of something special and unique.

As five o'clock comes and goes, I allow myself to shut things down and get ready to leave. I walk the halls of the arena, saying good night to staff as they head out. Saving the lower level for last, I see a few guys in with the trainers. I pass Devon's office, hopeful, only to find it dark. I've missed her.

I miss her.

24
9 ½ weeks

Devon

A nurse in cat-printed scrubs squirts goo on a tool that looks like a long, skinny vibrator. She chatters incessantly, as if I'm not lying here, spread-eagle, totally exposed to her.

"Once, I inserted the vaginal ultrasound tool and, boy, I pulled that thing out faster than you can say lickety-split," she chatters away as she inserts the tool into me. "I told the patient, *there's a baby in there*, and she was like, *yeah, no duh, I'm pregnant.* I was like, *no, I mean a baby-baby. Like, not a fetus. A baby.* So, I switched to the belly and sure enough, there was a whole baby in there. She was, like, twenty-five weeks along!"

"Is that possible?" I ask. "To not know you're pregnant for that long?"

"It doesn't happen often, but she said she didn't think she could get pregnant. She hadn't had a period in over a year, so it wasn't a big deal that she didn't have her cycle. And she was heavier set, so she didn't look pregnant so much. She said she never got sick or anything." She lifts a shoulder.

I turn my head to the little black-and-white screen. There, illuminated proof of what I already know. A tiny, gummy bear-looking thing. Not a baby-baby as she just described, but what will become one.

"Well, there you have it. Looks pretty healthy so far." She does some things on the machinery below the screen, then removes the ultrasound wand. "About nine and a half weeks, it seems. Does that sound right?"

I nod, tears stinging in my eyes. Yes, that matches up to my night in the hotel with Grant. A little, living blob inside of me. Oh God, what am I going to do?

"I'll step out so you can get dressed, then we'll have you chat with the doctor."

She slips out of the exam room, and I sit myself up, unable to process. Numb and shocked, I manage to dress myself, but I am on total autopilot. When I exit the exam room, the nurse leads me to the doctor's office. I follow her blindly, barely able to do much more than put one foot in front of the other, my mind spinning with so many thoughts and questions. The first and foremost being: *How am I going to do this?*

I'm having a baby.

Correction, Pearson, you're having Grant's baby.

"So, Devon Pearson," the doctor says, looking up

from my chart. Dr. O'Hara is a pretty redhead. She has a warmth about her that instantly comforts me. "From the look of you, I take it this is an unplanned pregnancy?"

I nod, unable to do any more than that just yet.

"I understand. It happens, of course. I see it frequently in my line of work. Come's with the job."

"Of course. And he told me the condom leaked a bit. But he thought he couldn't...well, it's complicated."

Dr. O'Hara gives me an empathetic look. "These things can be complicated. Humans are complicated. And you have time to decide, of course. Not much, but some."

"Time to decide what?" I ask, confused. Then it dawns on me, and I suck in a breath, sitting up a little straighter. "Oh. No, I—I don't want to do *that*. I'm having this baby."

A sharp nod as the doctor writes on her prescription pad. "Okay, then. Here is a script for prenatal vitamins. We'll see you back for your twelve-week check-up when you're safely through the first trimester. Do you want the ultrasound photos?"

"I do."

Not ten minutes later, I'm back in my car, staring at the photographic evidence that I am going to be a mother.

And Grant is going to be a father, even though he has no idea.

I have to get to work. Forcing myself to breathe in and out, in and out, I manage to tamp down the panic that threatens to overwhelm me. After I get on the road, I call Gia.

"So what's the verdict?" she asks immediately.

"Eleven weeks from the last period. Which means it was nine and a half weeks since the conference, just like the movie in the eighties."

"So definitely a conference baby, then."

"Yes."

"Will you keep it?"

"Of course," I say sharply.

"Whoa, there, tiger. Just asking."

"I'm sorry, I'm just in shock. And I don't know what to do, you know? I'm pregnant by a man I can't have an open relationship with. I'm trying to launch my own business. It just—it just feels like it can't get any worse."

"Will you tell him?" Gia asks.

I let out a long sigh. "I don't know. Maybe after the season gets started? He doesn't need this stress right off the bat. He's making a bunch of staffing changes and he doesn't need something like this to worry about."

"Wow," Gia says. Then, "Seriously?"

"What?"

"It takes two to tango, Dev. You have a job and a side business. He's not the only one with stuff going on. Why are you bearing the full weight of something that affects you both? Plus, he seems like the kind of guy who'd want to know."

"Of course, you're right. He said he wants kids—er, wanted kids. He tried with his ex but they never got pregnant. She got pregnant right away with her new boyfriend, so Grant thought maybe he couldn't...you know."

"He thought his swimmers couldn't swim," Gia confirms. "Damn. Sounds like that bitch was doing some trickery on the poor guy. How is that even possible?"

"I don't know. And it doesn't matter. I just need to think."

"You'll figure it out, girl. You're fierce and smart and self-sufficient."

"I'm a capable person," I say with a confidence I barely feel. "I can handle this."

"Hell yeah, you can." Gia says. "And your best friend will be at your side the whole way."

"God, I needed to hear that, Gia."

"Of course, I'll be there, Dev. We're a team."

"Thank you. Love you."

"Love you back." *Thank God for Gia.*

I GET to my office and plunge myself into work. Players are trickling back from their summer breaks, and I've got lots of nutrition meetings lined up.

Apparently, Grant is asking all players to be on a nutrition and fitness plan. He wants every player in top shape, all working out just as hard at third-string as they would if they were playing in starting positions.

My busy day flies by, and it's not until late in the afternoon that I have a minute to run down to the therapy gym to drop off some notes to Pam.

"Hey, girl," she says as she massages the hamstring of one of the guys. "What's up?"

"Just dropping some notes for you to review."

"Okay. How's you? Busy now that the guys are all back?"

"Yep, yep, it's getting real busy," I say. "You?"

"Just gettin' back in the swing," she answers. "Loosening folks up. Trying to get used to being a working mom."

"Yeah? How are things with the kids?"

Pam's radiant smile says it all. "Christ, for two people who always said they never wanted babies, we sure love having kids. They were, like, made for us."

"And Tyler? Is he involved? Is his mom?"

"Tyler's always around, which is awesome. He and Zoya are the best uncle and auntie any two kiddos ever had. The mom who birthed them?" She grimaces and shakes her head. "She took off once she signed away her rights at the settlement hearing. Straight up disappeared. Georg and I are committed to always being honest about the kids' lives before they came to us, but thankfully they stopped asking about her a while ago."

"That's probably for the best then, but I'm sorry."

"Small price to pay. Seriously. They're so great and Georg is totally smitten. It's the best thing ever seeing him be a dad."

"I'm happy for you both."

"So when will Devon Pearson settle down and make ridiculously beautiful babies?" she asks with typical Pam cheekiness.

Sooner than you think. "Oh, I don't know." I shrug and give her an Academy Award-worthy smile, and wave goodbye.

AS I FINISH out the workday down in my office, I realize I made it through these last eight hours better than I thought I might when I first arrived this morning.

Throwing myself into my work and focusing on my priorities of the moment has helped me to find some clarity with my situation.

So, I've made the decision I'll wait until after my next appointment to tell Grant about the baby. I need to tell him; there's no question. I doubt he'll be all that upset because I know he wants kids. And I believe he'll make a wonderful dad. Grant is a good man. He'll want to do the right thing and be supportive, I'm sure.

But I don't want the "right thing" to rock the boat for him so early in his tenure here. There's too much going on, and he has too much to prove to the organization as a whole.

I'll let him get the season started.

And I'll get past the twelve-week mark.

We'll talk about it then.

25
big gestures of love?

Grant

"I'm liking what I'm hearing," Max is saying. "The new coaching acquisitions seem solid, and I love the enhanced nutrition and training programming."

"I just hope it all pays off. I took a few risks, but people seem to be on board for the most part."

"Well, I can't complain. I asked for new ideas and you're giving them to me. There's more buzz and energy around this place than I've seen in a while. I'm happy to see some real effort being put forth toward players beyond the starting lineup."

"It's the future," I tell him. "Those guys are great. They're a high-functioning unit and they're leaders to the rest of the team, but they won't be around forever. It's just the way of the game."

And it is. I'm a perfect example of this reality. Players can be on the top of their games and have it taken away with one injury. It's the risk we take as athletes, and while it's sad to see a great player injured or forced into retirement, the game is still a business, and the business needs to be sustainable beyond its superstars.

After I finish with Max, I take a walk down to the training rooms. Dale, our head fitness trainer, is spotting rookie forward Aiden Kennedy, as he works at the squat rack.

"How's it going in here?" I announce my presence from the doorway.

Aiden grunts as he squats and pushes back up. With a laugh, Dale says, "Well, Aiden is probably going to put a voodoo curse on me after today's workout, but otherwise, we're good."

Aiden snorts. "Dude, I went to Yale. No voodoo there."

"Okay, well then, whatever kind of curse snobby rich people put on people, it's probably coming my way."

I can't help but grin at the banter. I miss this part of being a player the most. Well, besides playing the game. I miss having a group of guys that feels like a family. Being in management always makes me feel just a step away from it all, a bit removed. I think that's why I was so excited to come here. I'd heard there was this kind of magic happening in Vegas, and I see it every day. It extends beyond just the relationships between the players.

"You know, Bud never really came down here," Dale says as Aiden works through his next set of squats.

"I can't say much about Bud, but I do like to know the staff and see what they're doing for the team. I'm hearing great things about the training and nutrition programming, though."

"Yeah, Devon and I make a good team," Dale says.

I have to stop myself from physically reacting to his comment. It's harmless. It's a compliment to the work they do together, but it makes my blood boil, the thought of anyone making a good team with Devon.

My Devon, the possessive part of my brain bellows at him.

Except she's not mine. She's made it clear that she doesn't want to keep crossing the line with me. It's that thought that calms me. If she won't cross the line with me, then she sure won't do it with Dale.

I excuse myself with a, "Keep up the good work," before heading down the hall to the therapy gyms. Pam, a blonde ray of sunshine, smiles as I walk in.

"Hey!" she exclaims. "I'm so glad to see you."

I look over my shoulder and point to myself questioningly.

"Yeah, you," she says. "I've been asking for new equipment since the day I got here. My requisition was, like, floating out in space somewhere awaiting Bud's signature for who knows how long. You get here and, boom, my stuff shows up. If I wasn't married and you weren't my boss, I'd kiss you."

"Well, I'll settle for you being happy."

"You are a man who gets things done. I respect that."

"Happy to help where I can. All going well down here?"

Pam nods. "It's early so we're just working on old injuries now. Loosening the guys up."

"Good to hear. Let's hope we don't have a high injury season." I knock on a nearby wood table.

She crosses her fingers and holds them up. "I do like the focus you're putting on health and fitness. When I was first hired, it was like *Animal House* up in here. The guys partied constantly. Half their sweat during games was probably vodka. They fought, and sometimes each other. It was kind of a shitshow, pardon my French."

"I've heard, but things seem to have settled down on their own."

"They have, but this is like the 2.0 version. They're in love with winning and they want to keep doing it, so they've realized that they can't just rest on their talent alone. They must keep working, keep getting better. Keep working *together*."

"That's always the way. We have to keep getting better."

"For what it's worth, I think you're just the right person to help make that happen. I don't know if anyone's told you this, but Bud was rather absent. He bumbled around here and there, but he wasn't engaged with any of us. I'm not certain he could have remembered my name—even after I danced around in a bunny costume on the ice."

Caught off guard, I let out a surprised laugh. Pam winks and says, "We like big gestures of love around here, Grant."

"I'll keep that in mind," I say, still grinning. "And I keep hearing that my predecessor wasn't as active as he could or should have been. I don't really want to disparage a man I haven't met, so I think maybe let's just focus on the future?"

"Sounds good, boss." Pam grins, giving a mock salute.

I head out in the direction of Devon's office after leaving Pam in the therapy suite. I know I should just walk on by, but it's not like I have much choice when it comes to her. I do a lot of things differently where Devon Pearson's concerned, and right now, I need to lay my eyes on her again, even if it's just to reassure me she's here. When I see her light on, I pause for only a second before stepping into her doorway. She's concentrating at her desk, which means I can look at her without her knowing I'm here. I notice the dark circles under her eyes first. *Is she not sleeping?* My level of concern only rises when I notice how pale she looks.

"Hey there," I say quietly. Still, she jumps. "That

was my attempt not to startle you. You looked like you were concentrating pretty hard."

Devon sits up in her seat and adjusts the cardigan she's wearing, pulling it tightly around her midsection. "Hey there, to you. Just looking over some bloodwork for one of the guys."

"Everything okay?"

"Yeah, routine testing of cholesterol, triglycerides, and so on. Our nutrition programming is all based on their individual body chemistries, so I'm trying to make sure everything is in line. We'll retest on red flag areas once we've been at it for a few months."

"I'm hearing really amazing things about what you're all doing down here. Your name comes up often. In a good way. Can I sit?"

Devon hesitates but then nods. "I've got a player coming in soon."

I can hear the warning in her voice, and I don't blame her. It's awkward between us right now, but that spark is still there. I can feel it in every molecule of my body, and I want nothing more than to kiss her here and now, damn anyone who walks in on us.

Taking a seat, I ask, "You doing okay?"

She nods but there's no energy in it. "I'm fine."

"You look tired," I say as gently as possible. "Burning the candle at both ends?"

"I assure you my work here is getting done," she says with an edge to her voice. "I'm not doing side work while I'm here."

"That wasn't the point of the question. I know you're doing good work here. I just remarked how you get compliments all the time. The guys love what you're doing for them. You're a rock star nutritionist. But you look like you haven't been sleeping."

"Well, I've had some things on my mind." She looks away. To me, it looks purposeful, like she doesn't want me to know what *things* have been on her mind.

"You know, I'm here if you want to talk. Always."

"Thanks." She looks down at her lap and then quickly back to the computer screen.

I sit for a few more beats before pushing up out of the chair. "Devon, I really miss talking to you."

She looks up at me, and I can see the pain behind her eyes, but she doesn't say anything in return.

"Why don't you let me take you to dinner?" I suggest. "We'll grab a bite and talk about how things are going with your side gig?"

"I don't think that's the best idea, Grant, and you know why."

"Don't say someone might notice us or some other garbage. I need to see you."

Her beautiful mouth opens, then closes again. "I have class tonight."

"Then we'll set something up for later this week. Devon, I can't—I can't pretend I don't want to see you."

She's quiet for a long stretch of time, but finally, she speaks. "Later in the week, then."

I can't help my sigh of relief. "I'll text you."

As I step out into the hallway, I realize one of our younger players is right outside the door, waiting for me to exit. I give him a nod and walk toward the elevator, hoping he didn't hear too much of that conversation.

Shit. So much for being clandestine. The rumor mill is sure to blow up if he heard and interpreted our conversation the right way.

As I step onto the elevator, I feel such a sudden pang of sadness. *This is ridiculous.*

I really care about this woman, and I shouldn't have to sneak around with someone I genuinely care about, like she's my dirty little secret. Other people have relationships around here. Why can't I? I'm going to talk to Max. Devon and I are a good fit for each other, and it's so foolish to deny that. I know the difference between something that's good and something that's not worth pursuing. *I lived the latter.* I don't agree that people will think I sleep with "staff" if I'm in a relationship with Devon.

And I'll talk to Devon about my plan when we go to dinner.

I'm done with this shit. *Fuck it.*

Fuck. This. Shit. For real.

First, though, I'm heading to a cooking class tonight.

26

code for "you look terrible"

Devon

"Dev, don't take this the wrong way, but you look like doo-doo," Gia informs me as she counts out meal prep containers and places them at each seat.

"How could I possibly take that wrong, friend?" I shoot her a glare. "For the record, Grant was in my office today and said I looked tired. Isn't that code for *you look terrible*?"

"It was probably his way of expressing concern," Gia says.

"Well, he made a comment about how I must be burning the candle at both ends and I about knocked his head off. I feel kinda bad for snapping at him." I cringe at the memory.

"Baby hormones?"

"Ugh. I guess? My morning sickness is off the charts. I feel like total rot for about the first four hours of every day. It's messing with my own nutrition and fitness."

"It," Gia says flatly. "You mean, the living being inside of you?"

"*It,* meaning the state of being pregnant. I hear it'll get better during the second trimester, though."

"I sure hope so, because I hate running by myself."

Folks start to file in for class. The couples aren't here tonight, as this class is focused on lunchtime meal prep, so it's a decidedly less sexy topic. But the die-hard performers and athletes are still hanging in there with me, and Gia is happy to take her place back with Mikhail when he arrives. I watch them interact and find myself interested in how much chemistry they seem to have. Gia's been quiet about this thing with the Crush winger, and while I've expected her to lose interest already, it hasn't happened. I have to wonder if whatever's going on between them is more than just sex. Only time will tell.

I'm so busy thinking about Gia's love life that I nearly miss it when Grant walks in and takes a seat. It's been a couple of weeks since he's been to class. Well, two weeks, in fact, since I went to his house, slept with him, and then told him to stay away. Not that I'm counting or anything. He's also shit at following instructions.

As I start class, I can definitely feel the weight of his stare again, same as the last time he came here. He's as intense as always, but when I see his brow furrow, I realize just how observant Grant is. He saw it earlier, when he asked if I was okay, and I can tell he's picking up on something now. Damn.

Maybe I should tell him tonight?

Or not.

I just don't know.

I focus back on the immediate task at hand. "So today we're talking about meal prep for lunchtime. Chicken is like a perfect lean meat. You can't get much better, really, but a lot of times, it can get really dry, especially if it's in the fridge for a few days. So we're going to work on prepping and cooking the chicken so that it stays juicy through the week. And then we'll talk about different ways to prep your lunches so that you get some variety and aren't eating the same boring salad every damn day at lunch time."

This gets a few chuckles out of the crowd.

"Meal prep doesn't have to be a nightmare. Honestly, it's an hour of work now to keep you from making mistakes through the week. Those mistakes can really derail your nutritional goals, so you've got to think about this like an appointment. You make working out part of your routine, so think about prepping meals the same way."

I have everyone pull out the chicken from their station refrigerators and we talk through how to prep it. The feel and look of the raw chicken make my stomach queasy, though. So much so that I have to turn away, close my eyes, and take a deep breath. I power through the instructions, and as everyone is working, I excuse myself to the restroom, barely making it into the small space before throwing up.

God, I hope no one heard that. Nothing less appetizing than trying to cook while someone is puking twenty feet away.

I heave through it, then swish some water around in my mouth and spit it out before washing my hands. I suck in a few deep breaths and then go back out to the classroom. But as soon as I return to my station and see the gelatinous, pink meat sitting there, I break out into a cold sweat, my vision going blurry.

From far away, it seems like I can hear someone ask if I'm okay, but I feel wobbly, and my mouth is dry. I hold up a hand...just before everything goes black.

THERE'S a high-pitched buzzing in my ears as I blink back to consciousness. It takes a few seconds to get my bearings as my vision clears, Grant and Gia's worried faces hovering above me. I look around and try to sit up, confused. Oh my God, did I just faint in front of my class?

"Don't try to sit up." Gia presses me gently back. "Grant's just called for an ambulance."

"Oh my God, why would he do that?"

"You hit your head pretty hard," my friend says.

I hear a commotion coming from the back as Grant stands and barks at someone, "She's back here."

I try to sit up a second time, but Grant says, "Stay put. You're bleeding."

My sheer mortification intensifies as the EMS crew comes in with a stretcher. They put a neck brace on me, take my pulse, ask a few questions.

"Can you tell us your name?"

"Uh, Devon Pearson," I say, cringing. "Ow, my head hurts."

"Do you remember what happened?"

"I went to the restroom and then I came back out and—"

"You turned white as a ghost before passing out," Gia finishes for me. "Scared the crap out of everyone in the room."

"Sorry, everyone," I say.

"Well, we're going to put you on the stretcher and take you to get checked out," one of the paramedics says. "You've hit your head pretty hard."

"I don't—I'm fine—" I start throwing up again, but there's not a lot left in me to come up.

"Clearly you're totally fine," Gia says dryly. "Not a concussion or anything like that."

"Jerk," I grumble as the paramedics load me onto the stretcher. When they lift me up, I'm horribly embarrassed by the whole thing that's happening here tonight. An entire room full of people just watched me totally wipe out and then, to top it off, by puking on the classroom floor for the grand finale. They'll probably never come back. My side gig is probably officially over.

"I'm sorry," I say as I pass by my students with worried faces. "I'll make this up to you all. I'll refund you for this week's class."

"Don't be ridiculous," I hear someone say. "Feel better."

Gia climbs in the back of the ambulance and holds my hand as they start the engine. The last thing I see before they shut the doors is Grant's worried face.

27
told me what?

For however long I've been pacing this waiting room floor, it feels like fucking forever.

I head to the nearest nurses' station. Again. "Please, can you give me an update on my friend? Devon Pearson?"

"Sorry." Nurse Julie shakes her head at me. "You're not listed as family or an emergency contact, Mr. Gerard. Unless she consents, we can't share any information."

"Well, her friend is back there. Will you at least go ask her friend Gia to come out and talk to me?"

They say they'll pass along the message, so I head back to a row of seats and shove myself into the chair, legs bouncing nervously. I send probably the fourteenth text to Devon, asking if she's okay.

When tiny, pixie-haired Gia comes out, she points

at me in annoyance. "You. Slow your roll. Stop texting an injured woman. She needs to rest."

"Well, no one will tell me what is going on. I'm worried about her, okay?"

"Well, I'm here now. And she's okay. She just needed fluids. She was dehydrated."

"Oh." I let out a breath of utter relief. "That's it? And her head?"

"Couple of stitches. She's probably mildly concussed but nothing significant."

"Can I please see her?"

"Sure. As long as you're not going to be all *extra* about it."

"Extra? Me?"

Gia lifts one eyebrow.

"Fine." I throw my hands up in surrender. "Calm as a cucumber over here."

"Isn't it *cool as a cucumber*?" Gia directs a calculated smirk in my direction. I get the distinct feeling she knows way more than she's telling. "Come on, lover boy, I'll take you, but remember what I said. Chill is the way to play this."

Oh-kay.

Chill is the way to play this?

Whatever that fuckin' means. I have no idea what is going on with Devon, but I feel like something is. I don't get into it with Gia, either. I'm so done with the cryptic vibe of bullshit everyone keeps feeding me. I need to see Devon, and I need to see her right the fuck now before I expire from worry. So, I keep my mouth shut and nod once, following Gia back into the patient rooms, knowing every step I take brings me that much closer to Devon.

She looks up at me, and her eyes fill with tears the second I come into her room. "Devon?" I can't get to her fast enough. But when I take her hand, the tears start spilling. I gently touch the bandage on her head. "Does it hurt? Are you in a lot of pain? You really scared me."

She shakes her head, eyes closed as tears still slip down her splotchy but still beautiful face. "It's just a cut. And I'm b-b-barely c-c-concussed."

"Shh, it's okay." I reach down and put my arms around her, just grateful to have her close again. Visibly upset and crying, yes, but she's conscious, and from all accounts, not seriously injured. "What, then? Can you tell me? I want to help."

A doctor interrupts us, trailing a medical equipment cart along behind him as she pulls herself out of my arms.

"Devon Pearson." He greets her with a professional smile. "Okay to get started with your visitor in the room, or would you like a little privacy?"

I look from him to the cart and back to Devon again as she shakes her head. "It's fine. He can be here. I just haven't told him yet."

"Told me what?" I feel the hair on the back of my neck stand straight up at the odd sound of her voice.

Devon's hand slips from mine and she rests it on her abdomen. "That I'm"—she shakes her head and frowns—"no, that *we* are pregnant."

Time stops.

Just...fucking...grinds...to...a...dead...halt.

The earth stops spinning in its orbit around the sun.

I know I forget to breathe, just like I know my mouth is hanging down to the floor like a cartoon character in shock.

And when the record starts to spin again, I feel my eyes get hot with tears. *She's PREGNANT?*

The doctor moves over and has Devon lift her gown, exposing what I now see as the smallest little swell of a baby bump. He squirts some gel onto her skin and turns on the machine, pressing the wand end against her stomach. A whooshing sound fills the stunned silence between us as we look at the black-and-white image on the screen.

"We're having a baby." I breathe, still processing the news.

"Yes, we are." She gives me a smile that's a mix of half-happy and half-worry before I jolt with panic. "When you fell, it didn't—I mean, you're okay, right? Everything looks okay, right?"

Devon peers at the screen. "The blob looks a little different than it did last time, but heck, I don't know. Is that what it's supposed to look like at this stage?"

The doctor chuckles. "Well, first, you're not having *a baby*."

My heart drops. "What do you mean?"

He grins. "You're having two babies. Twins. See, there are two distinct little bodies in there, and each one has its own healthy heartbeat."

As he points out each feature, I start to see the outline of two little people. They look like tiny candy bears. Devon looks as dumbfounded as I feel.

"I'm sure there was only one at the last ultrasound," she says shakily. "They can't just multiply in the womb, right?"

Laughing, the doctor assures us both. "No. Sometimes we can't identify multiples early on. One fetus might be hiding behind the other in early images. As they get bigger and need more room, they usually reveal themselves. Honestly, this is probably why you've had such horrible morning sickness. The more hormones in your system, the sicker you are, in most cases. Also, this makes your pregnancy slightly higher risk. But everything looks fine and good, and you appear to be the picture of twenty-eight-year-old health. Nothing to worry about from the fall. I'll get you some discharge paperwork, as well as a referral to a high-risk specialist. Dr. Reilly is excellent if you decide to go with him."

He finishes the ultrasound, printing off a few of the grainy, black-and-white images and handing them to me before wiping the goo off Devon's belly. On his way out, he offers a congenial, "Congratulations, Mom and Dad."

We sit in stunned silence for a few moments, holding hands. Finally, Devon speaks, asking timidly, "Are you upset with me?"

"Why would I be upset with you?" I'm genuinely confused.

"Because I didn't tell you. And I pushed you away." Devon's eyes fill with tears again.

I scoot closer to her, leaning in, my forehead touching hers. "No. I'm not upset."

"Are you sure? I plan on having them, but I won't —wouldn't ask you to—"

I stop her speech with a kiss.

As I sit back, I use my thumb to wipe away her tears under each eye. "Devon, I couldn't be happier. This is the best news I've ever heard."

"Really? But this just makes things so much more complicated."

"What's complicated about it? I've always wanted kids. I'd just about given up on it because I didn't think it was possible. And I care for you. You care for me. We're really good together. We're going to be the best parents ever and make a beautiful family."

"Grant, us caring about each other doesn't make our work situation go away. We met for the first time barely three months ago. And let's be honest, it won't be you who loses your job over this. You're the new golden boy, the whiz kid manager who's doing everything right. They can find a new nutritionist much easier than they can find a great GM."

"*I* can't replace you, though," I say firmly. "I value your work and I'll walk if they try to fire you. Besides, what kind of bullshit double standard would that be? It takes two to tango, as they say. Plus, we met before I started here."

The more I speak, the more impassioned I become. We haven't done a thing wrong. Our relationship—and yes, I'm calling it a relationship—started before we became employees. *I'm deliriously fuckin' happy.* "We didn't do anything wrong, as you've said, my beautiful Devon. I'll fight for you. For us." *For my children. Fuck.*

Devon, still teary, doesn't seem all that convinced. "This pregnancy is high-risk; you heard the doctor. I don't want to be stressed-out at work, worried what people are saying and thinking. I want to be calm and healthy for the babies. I don't want something bad to happen."

I lean in and kiss her again. And even though we're in a hospital and the news is a lot to take in, the feeling of her lips beneath mine calms me. This feels like home to me. Like everything is clicking into place as it should.

"Nothing bad is going to happen. I will not allow it." I hold her cheeks in my hands. "Devon, I would be devastated if anything happened to you or these babies, so I hear you. But I need you to hear me when

I say this will be okay. Better than okay. And we'll figure it out together. It's going to be fine. I promise. Please don't worry for a moment. I'm going to take care of all of you and I'll keep repeating it until you believe me. I'm going nowhere. I'm here to take care of all three of you."

"You are?" she whispers, her dark brown eyes filling with new tears for me to wipe away again.

"I wouldn't have it any other way, my gorgeous, twin-baby mamma," I whisper back before kissing every tear from her beautiful face.

More fiercely than I've ever felt anything in my life, *I know this.*

28
scandalizing the neighbors

Devon

I've been up since dawn, obsessing over budget worksheets. I woke up feeling sick and anxious, worried about how I can have two babies and two jobs and a baby daddy who can't tell anyone he's my baby daddy.

I sent Grant away after getting home from the hospital last night. He helped me to the couch, got me some water, and sat with me for a long time. We didn't talk much. Instead, I just put my head on his shoulder and held his hand, comforted by his presence. Grant is a big man. He's tall and broad and manly, but seeing him reduced to tears when he learned he'd be a father? It only confirmed what I already knew about him in my heart—Grant Gerard is the best of men. The kind of man I want to have with me on this journey.

However, it's never just that simple. We still work together. We still need to think about how we'll navigate what could be an embarrassing and stressful situation for both of us. I found myself thinking a lot about whether I could walk away from the Crush and seriously throw myself into my own business. And at some point, after we got back from the hospital, I felt exhausted and needed some space to rest and think, so I told Grant I needed to be alone and sent him home. I know he wanted to stay with me, but I just needed some solitude to process all the thoughts swirling in my head. A little space to begin to sort through and figure things out.

So here I am, in the tank top and underwear I wore to bed, my hair piled in a rat's nest on top of my head, glasses perched on my nose. I did sleep some, but I tossed and turned a whole lot more. When I couldn't stand it anymore, I got out of bed and pulled up my budget spreadsheets, looking for a clear message that perhaps I could leave my full-time job and set out on my career journey on my own—earlier than planned.

The doorbell rings, pulling me from my assessments. At this hour, it's probably just Gia coming by to check on me before setting out on her morning run. I shuffle to the door and swing it open, but it's not Gia I find at my doorstep.

It's Grant, looking as mouthwatering as ever in black athletic shorts, a Crush T-shirt, and running shoes.

It's Grant also looking rather surprised by the sight of me answering the door, barely dressed.

His eyes darken, sweeping every inch of my body, from my bare feet to the messy pile on top of my head. My whole body tingles, and I feel my cheeks heat under his scrutiny. Rooted in place, I'm unable to move simply from the intensity of his stare.

"Why do you always seem so shocked at how you affect me?" he asks, the back of his finger tracing what I assume is the blush covering my cheeks.

At a loss for words, I stammer, saying something about looking like shit, not sleeping very well, and working on budget spreadsheets. I end my lame-ass rambling with an even lamer, "I don't know."

Grant leans in and whispers, "Well, then." Suddenly he's closed the gap between us, one of his hands at the base of my neck, the other at the small of my back. He kisses me, and I melt, my body instantly sinking into him, feeling the press of an erection growing behind his shorts. "You're so fuckin' sexy to me. Dressed up or just out of bed, you're a goddess. I want you so badly, all the fucking time," he growls against my ear between urgent kisses.

The sound of a throat-clearing has us pulling apart quickly, like two teenagers caught making out by their parents. I look over Grant's shoulder to find my elderly neighbor, clearly shocked by our indecent display. "Sorry, Mrs. Winters." Hiding behind Grant's big body, we shimmy quickly inside my apartment, shutting the door with a bang.

I can't help but giggle. "We just scandalized poor Mrs. Winters. I hope she's okay."

"Well, it's probably the most action she's seen in a long time." Grant's grin is absolutely devilish.

"It was quite the show." I purse my lips at him.

"We probably could've done better, though." He licks his lips at me.

I cock my head at him coyly. "Guess we'd better keep practicing, then."

Not missing a beat, Grant has me pressed against the wall again, kissing me—no, more like devouring me with wild kisses. I can hardly get enough as I cling to him, my hands grasping at his shirt, desire blooming in my belly. He hauls me up into his strong arms and carries me into my bedroom, where my blankets and sheets remain rumpled from my restless night. Grant pushes everything out of the way and lays me on the bed, pushing my tank top up to bare my breasts, my nipples already rock hard, jutting shamelessly for attention.

"God, you're perfect," he murmurs against my skin, mouthing and teasing at my sensitive, swollen breasts until I'm arching and moaning and nearly ready to come just from this small bit of busy attention.

Grant's fingers play first along the outside of my soft cotton boy shorts, but it's not long before he slips beneath to tweak my clit, feeling the slippery wetness gathering already between my folds. My hips push up to meet his ministrations, nearly begging for his fingers to sink inside me.

I'm moaning nonsensical sounds, feeling wild but tamed, held in his strong arms while he works me to a frenzy. My clit pulsating harder the closer I soar toward my impending climax, my inner walls tightening almost violently around his fingers.

Still holding two long fingers deep inside me, my whole body stiffens. I forget to breathe. The orgasm he forces from me begins to overtake all my senses.

Grant stares into my eyes as he makes me come—spectacularly and hard—pinned beneath him in my bed, fucked to within an inch of my life by his glorious, magical fingers.

I'm sure it was the best stress reliever, bar none, he could've given to me right now. *Thank you, sir, may I have another?* When I settle, he continues to kiss me deeply, literally devouring me with long, erotic kisses making me feel treasured and cherished.

"I want to make love to you, Devon," he says against my lips. "Is it safe?"

"I think so. Just be gentle?"

"Gentle wasn't where my mind was. Fuck, sorry. Your stitches?"

"Can't feel a thing." *Who knew orgasms could be better than pain medication?*

He smiles, and good God, is that a sinfully wicked smile he has in his arsenal. *No wonder I can't resist him.*

I watch as he peels away his clothing, first his shirt, baring his broad, toned chest and abs. I can't imagine ever not wanting to look at him, at his body. He just does things to me. Makes me feel safe and wanted. He makes me ache.

Naked, he crawls onto the bed, pulling my underwear down over my legs, another rakish grin on his face. "I've missed you," he says before dipping his head to kiss my belly.

Just the feel of his lips on my skin makes me moan. "I've missed you too," I tell him as he kisses his way to each of my breasts.

He continues trailing kisses up to my neck, over my jaw, to the shell of my ear, whispering hotly, "What do you want, Devon? Tell me what you want."

"You, Grant." I breathe. "I want you to make love to me like you said. I need to have you inside me right now."

"Don't have to mess with condoms anymore since I already knocked you up." He winks wickedly.

"Hmm, you're very proud of that fact. And here you thought your swimmers didn't swim. Twins though, Mr. Gerard. You're a damn stud," I tease him right back.

His eyes grow hooded as he stares down at me, his powerful body possessing mine, ready to fuck me. "This stud can't wait to be inside you bare, with nothing between us, just me"—he aligns the tip of his cock to my center—"and you," he grunts, filling me all the way up.

He claims my body in a way that's possessive and demanding, yet loving. I'm crying as he moves inside me, still kissing me deeply in a measured rhythm with the powerful thrusts of his cock deep into my depths.

My hands roam down the bare skin of his back, feeling the flexing muscles of his sculpted ass pumping into me. When I urge him to move faster, he laughs against my mouth. "What happened to gentle?"

"Maybe somewhere in the middle?"

Another chuckle as he picks up the pace, moving in and out in a tempo that creates such good friction, his pelvis striking just at the right spot. When I come, it's with such force that I lose my breath for a moment, stars exploding like fireworks on a summer night. Grant is right behind me with his own climax, his kisses growing harder, his tongue spearing into my mouth with more possession than before, if that's even possible.

A second orgasm immediately follows my first, a trek to the top of the tallest mountain, and then a fall from unimaginable heights. And when I cry out, Grant falls with me, roaring out his pleasure, still pinning me to the bed with his pounding cock, growling how good fucking me makes him feel, vowing he'll never stop fucking me, telling me how good my cunt feels coming around his cock.

It's a wild romp of sex and orgasms with my very

own dirty talker in the bedroom, whispering filthy things to me the whole wonderful way.

And it's everything I needed from him at this moment.

GRANT'S heartbeat thumps wildly beneath my cheek as I rest on his chest. It should be beating wildly. I think he just fucked me to within an inch of his life.

I loved every second of it, and I'm certain he did too.

He never stops touching me, stroking up and down my back with his fingertips, the sides of my breasts, the swell of a hip, causing my skin to erupt in gooseflesh. I'm so boneless afterward, it takes all my energy just to get up and head into the bathroom to clean up. Sex is definitely a lot messier without a condom.

Grant follows me in, wets a washcloth, takes to his knees, and gently cleans me. Then, he puts his hands at my hips and kisses the small swell of my belly. I expect this to be a quiet moment, a moment of reflection or of reverence, but instead, he buries his face between my legs, his tongue flicking against my ultra-sensitive clit, my already swollen folds. It's so sensitive, in fact, I nearly can't handle the sensations. I cry out, shaking my head, grasping at the countertop behind me. There is no purchase to be found, though, and I'm left helpless as he makes me come again and again.

When the climaxing finally stops, Grant stands, picks me up, and carries me back to bed. I know things shouldn't ever be said when you're basking in the aftereffects of orgasms, but for some reason, the bliss I'm feeling seems...safe. I feel *safe* in this man's arms, and I don't seem to have any doubts that if he says he'll stand by my side, then he will do exactly that.

29

peony on knight boulevard

"What day is it?" Devon asks, the vibrations rumbling through my chest.

She's against my side, her head on my chest, one leg crossed over mine. We're still naked, and I have no idea how long we've been lying here on her bed, naked. It could've been hours by now. My stomach growls in answer.

"Saturday. I think." I wiggle to my side so Devon is now on her back. Propped up with one hand, I lay my other on her belly. "I can't wait to see you getting bigger as they grow. I can't wait to feel them move inside of you."

"I hope we didn't scar them too much by what we just did," Devon says with a giggle. Her blush nearly makes me hard again. "I mean, is it weird that we've just had sex and there are two little lives inside of me?"

"It's amazing. A miracle. And honestly? The fact that you're having my babies only makes me want you more. Is that weird?"

My stomach growls again, loudly, and Devon laughs, sitting up. "Well, that's the second time your stomach has made its intentions known. And, frankly, I have a massive craving for Chinese takeout."

"Isn't it, like, breakfast time?"

"Babies want Chinese food," Devon growls, heading for her walk-in closet.

I admire the magnificent sight of her ass as she leaves, until it tragically disappears from my view, of course. It's hard to take my eyes off her at any time, but when she's naked? Impossible. *God, she's a beautiful woman. Mother of my children. Mine. No fuckin' corporate policy is going to change the facts or keep us apart while I have something to say about it.*

"Chinese it is then, boss." I do have enough functioning brain matter to know not to argue food choices with a pregnant woman. Not if I'd like to keep my balls intact for any possible sibling add-ons in the future.

Checking my phone, I confirm what I'd assumed. It's nearly lunchtime. No wonder everyone is hungry. I get dressed while Devon rattles off her order from the inside of her closet. "Peony on Knight Boulevard. Can you find it on your phone and do a DoorDash? I want the house special fried rice, corn egg-drop soup, the

Moo-Shoo pork, oh, and those chicken skewers they do that are to die for. I can't remember what they're called on the menu but don't forget them, please. Oh, and an order of veggie egg rolls...and oh yeah, anything else you'd like to add, Grant?"

"Um, I think what you've picked will be *plenty* of food for the two of us." I'm chuckling as I place the order from the delivery app, finding a ton of joy in the mundane task of over-ordering Chinese food for my woman because she's hungry and she wants it. Plus, the fact she's growing the two little humans we made together? Nothing at all complicated about wanting to take care of all three of them.

"Food's ordered. Says forty minutes, give or take on the app."

"Great, thank you."

"Hey, what were you working on when I showed up at your door this morning?" I remember to ask.

"Oh, come look." She sweeps out of her closet, now dressed in loose shorts and a hooded T-shirt from Pride week, I'm guessing since it's the Vegas Crush logo in rainbow colors, gesturing me to the table where her laptop and other papers are scattered about. "I've got four regular nutrition clients now. I do food shopping and meal prep for them, and I think they'll be long-term clients. The weekly class is also going well, assuming I didn't gross everyone out by throwing up and bleeding all over in front of them."

"People were just worried about you. They won't think a thing of it," I reassure her.

She shows me her budget spreadsheet, pointing out the long-term projections. "I can't sustain myself on this income yet. It's part-time work at best and even though my salary at the Crush isn't much, I can't let it go yet. I was hoping there'd be a different story here, but there's not. Plus, I need the health insurance until the babies are born. I'm finishing the cookbook, too, and that income should be a nice bonus, but if it doesn't sell, then I won't be asked to do another."

When she looks up at me, I can see the worry in her eyes. "Take a breath, please. No one is asking or expecting you to quit your job."

"You don't know that. Twins will—I'll get bigger faster. It'll be harder to hide earlier on in the pregnancy and I'm not a liar, Grant. I don't want to hide that they're yours."

"You won't *ever* have to do that," I say a bit more harshly than I mean to. I sit in the chair next to her and pull her hands into mine.

"Have you told Max Terry yet?" She still has that worried look in her eyes, which bothers me a lot more than it probably should. Suddenly, the greatest need to make every single one of her worries to fucking be gone overtakes everything else.

"No, not yet, but I've requested a meeting with him and I'd like for you to be there."

She closes her eyes and blows out a long breath. "I will if you think that's what's best."

"I do." I lean in and kiss her lightly. "I want to be here to calm your nerves, to care for you. I will not be off in the shadows, sneaking around. And I hear Max is a pushover for a good romance. So we'll tell him what happened. We'll explain how and when we met. It will be fine."

"You know, I can take care of myself," Devon says.

"I know you can. You're quite remarkable, and I don't want you to feel trapped or burdened. I just really want this. I want you. I want our children. And I want us to do this together."

"You know, you're being awfully kind about...well, about the fact that I hid this from you."

I bite my bottom lip as I think about it. "How long have you known?"

"Two weeks. And you just said you don't want me to feel trapped. Well, I didn't want you to feel trapped, either. I wanted to give you a chance to get your first season started...and me, well, to make it through my first trimester safely, and then I was going to tell you. I don't want you to worry I was never going to tell you. I'm not the kind of person who'd ever keep something so important from you."

"I know you're not," I say, squeezing her hands in mine.

"Grant, it happened literally the first night we met. The first time we were together. Everything felt so sudden because it *was*. And you'd just started to hit your stride at work. People think you walk on water over there. I didn't want to ruin your first big start in the NHL."

"I don't walk on water, Devon." It comes out probably too sharply. "It was my obsession with having children that ruined my marriage. It made me a shitty partner."

"I'm sure there's more to it than just your desire to start a family. And no one is perfect. Not one person. I don't expect that from you, Grant."

"Well, I think you're pretty perfect," I say, brushing a finger up her cheek. "When I first saw you, instead of leaving the bar as I was going to do, I walked over *to* you. There was nowhere else that I could go but straight to your side. You were literally the most beautiful woman I had ever seen. And I was so far out of the dating game. I figured I'd come across like some bumbling fool. But then we talked, and it was so natural. You were witty and fun, and we connected instantly, so easily."

"I don't want you to think I just…do that…because I don't."

"You don't what?"

"I don't *sleep* with random men I meet at hotel bars." It comes out hushed as a charming blush spreads up her cheeks.

The laugh I let out is more like a bark, a sharp noise that takes us both off guard. "I'm sorry. Forgive me. I'm not laughing at you. I didn't think that at all. I've never had that thought about you, not once. In fact, the only thing I was able to think about during the weeks afterward was how—" I take in a breath at the memory.

"Mind-blowing it was?" Devon finishes with a shy smile. "I felt the same. I mean, I've gone out a few times since my divorce, but I didn't try that hard. I figured if I had to try, then it wasn't what I was looking for, you know? And I worried that, well, I worried that the same thing might happen again, that I wouldn't be enough."

I can't help myself from growling as I lean in and kiss her again. "You are enough. You are more than enough. And this is real, Devon. For me, this is so fucking real." I was with Margot for over a decade, and although I know I loved her, I don't recall feeling so...intense about *her.* I desperately wanted a family, but was it really Margot I wanted? In contrast, in such a short period of time, Devon owns me.

Makes me wonder...*Am I falling in love with her, or am I already there?*

She opens up to me, her tongue flitting against my bottom lip as the heat between us flares to life once more. It's always like this with her though. If we're alone? There's not a chance in hell I'm keeping my hands off her. All I know is that she's all mine now. No matter how it shakes out with my job, Devon

Pearson and our babies she's growing within her beautiful body are *mine*.

When the doorbell rings, I groan and laugh at the same time.

"Pause that thought," she says, shoving her chair back and standing with a languid stretch. "Eating for three now."

30
the godfather

"**I** feel like I'm going to throw up," I say as we make our way along the carpeted hallway toward Max Terry's sprawling office.

I've never been up here. This place is for superstars. This is where player deals happen. This is not where a lowly nutritionist comes to beg for her job while explaining that she's pregnant with the brand-new GM's twin babies.

I stop short of the door, trying to control my breathing, trying not to puke on the pristine, gold and cream-colored carpet of the executive suites.

"No worrying please, because it's going to be fine." Grant takes my cheeks in his hands and plants a kiss on my forehead. "I promise."

Grant knocks and then steps in without awaiting an answer. As I make my way in behind him, I take in the floor-to-ceiling windows and the view of the city that comes with them. This beats my closet in the basement by a long shot.

When Max Terry stands, I'm caught off guard by how handsome and warm he is. He has a genuine smile as he steps from behind his desk, extending his hand to mine. He shakes my hand, then Grant's, and then beckons us both to take a seat on a white leather couch.

"Max, you remember Devon Pearson. Team nutritionist."

"Devon." Max greets me warmly. "It's so good to see you again. I'm embarrassed I haven't been down to compliment your work before this. I've heard such amazing things about the much-improved fitness and nutrition regimen Grant has prescribed for the team."

"Thanks so much. I really enjoy my work here. And Grant gives good direction. He knows exactly what he wants for the team."

Grant gives Max a few updates about the program and lets me share some of my most recent success stories. Max seems genuinely interested in the work I'm doing, and he lavishes compliments on Grant, congratulating him on his good leadership.

The nervousness in my stomach threatens to have me hurling all over this pristine space again. There is no way Max is going to be okay with us being together. No way. My knee starts to bounce, and I'm startled when Grant reaches over and takes my hand in his.

Max is surprised, too, judging by the way his

eyebrows shoot into his hairline. "What is this?" He gestures to our entwined hands.

"Max, I should have probably talked to you about this right away. I met Devon the same day you offered me this job. She was at a conference at my hotel, and we hit it off. We made a pact to not talk about work or exes at the time, and that seemed refreshing, but it also meant we never knew we were both employed by the Vegas Crush Organization. Not until I got here and took that first tour with you. I was...shocked, to put it mildly, finding her working *here* in Las Vegas, of all places. It was too late by that point when we realized the situation we were in."

"We tried not to take it any further, sir," I chime in.

"But we just found out we're having twins together," Grant adds. "It was unplanned and unexpected, but it happened, and I wanted you to hear it from us—the whole story—before it got shared around the rumor mill."

Max recovers himself and tilts back in his chair, chuckling. "Wow. That's some fast progress with the team, fast progress in the bedroom."

Grant tenses beside me, sitting up ramrod straight, his hand tightening around mine. I clear my throat and beat him to a response, saying, "I'm *sure* you didn't mean that quite like it came out, sir."

Max, to his credit, looks properly embarrassed. "Of course not. No. Please, I apologize. I just meant this all happened for the two of you, *very fast.*"

"If it's going to be a problem, I'll exit the position and let you hire someone else," Grant says tersely.

Max looks absolutely horrified at this prospect. "Why would I ask you to exit the position? Why would I want you to leave for that matter? You're doing a great job here."

"I've heard about the non-fraternization policy. I thought you might see your brand-new general manager flouting the rules as a problem."

Max chuckles. "Well, that policy got thrown out the window the minute Evan Kazmeirowicz about burned the world down to get to his wife, Holly. Oh, and then Pam did nearly get herself fired for having... relations...with Georg in the PT gym. Then later proposing in the most public way possible prior to a championship game. Oh, and then there was Viktor and Scarlett, now happily married parents. So, I'd say we've been able to let it slide when needed. Especially when it's the real deal. Who am I to interfere, you know?" He rubs his hands together and clasps them, leaning back in his chair. "So, this is the real deal?"

I let out a breath I didn't even know I was holding in pure relief. "Yes," I tell Max, almost wishing I could go over and kiss him on the cheek in grateful thanks.

"It *was* a surprise," Grant adds. "But a good one. And yes, it's real."

"Okay, then. You have my blessing, or whatever it was you were looking for."

"Thank you," we both say at the same time.

"Okay, now get back to work," he jokes, waving us on our way.

We leave his office, and we're halfway down the hallway when I break into hysterical laughter.

"What?" Grant asks.

"That was like a scene out of *The Godfather*." I can't stop laughing. "How bizarre was that meeting just now?"

"That was a bit weird. You know I had the same thought about just coming up here and asking *The Godfather* for his blessing myself."

"You did?" I laugh at him.

"Mm-hmm." Grant has his hands in his pockets and his head tilted curiously as he takes in my strange emotional outburst. I'm nearly crying from laughter, and I can't figure out if it's humor, relief, or what, but somehow, all the crazy emotions I've been experiencing feel like they're lifting. It's like I can finally breathe without having to worry about losing my full-time job.

So, when Grant pushes me against the wall and crashes his lips down onto mine, I nearly forget that we actually *are* at work.

Nearly. But with more giggling, I do manage to push him back. "He said we had his blessing, not that we could make out in the hallway while we're on the clock, Grant Gerard, you cad."

Grant laughs and takes me by the hand. "Fair enough." He walks me the rest of the way down to the elevators, where he presses the down button for me. His office is up here on the executive floor, so this elevator will be my ride only. When it arrives, and I step in, he smacks my ass playfully. "Now get back to work."

31

quit being so emo

Grant

One week later.

Since our meeting with Max, there's been no "coming out" for my relationship with Devon, but it's certainly not a secret anymore. Word is out there making the rounds, I'm pretty sure.

Marielle is the first to succumb to curiosity, though, when I find her lingering at the doorway after delivering the mid-morning coffee.

"Something you need?"

She opens her mouth, then pinches it shut. "No, I…"

"That doesn't sound like an actual no, so out with it."

"It's just that I heard something, and I guess I'd rather know the truth from you than engage the rumor mill."

"So, ask."

"You won't be offended, I hope. I heard that you might have gotten a staff member pregnant here. And it's certainly not my business, and the person could have been mistaken. I just, well, I thought you'd want to know what people are saying."

I take a deep breath and count to ten. A useful trick my sister and I had ingrained into us by our always rational, no-nonsense mother, who even managed to keep her cool when she wanted to take someone's head off. I have a feeling I might need to call on such restraint.

"Here's the truth, Marielle. I met Devon Pearson before I knew she worked here, when I was in town interviewing for this job. I was shocked to find out she was employed by VCO, and we tried very hard not to make a thing of it. However, we really care about each other. And, yes, she is pregnant. We've spoken to Max Terry about it, so it's no big secret scandal or anything."

"Oh," she breathes. "You know, a lot of different types of men and women have worked here. And things do happen from time to time. I just didn't see you like that. To be one of those types of people."

"The type who sleep with the staff you mean?"

She gives me a small, rueful smile. "Yeah, that type."

"Well, I'm not, but I liked her before I knew we'd be working together. I won't apologize for it."

"I'm not asking you to apologize. It's just, do you think people will think differently of you for this?"

The fuck? I feel my face twist up, and I can't decide if I'm angry, amused, or annoyed. Maybe a little of all three? "Marielle, I'm in a relationship with a woman I care about deeply. I've always wanted to be a father, and I'm thrilled that we're making a family together. Yes, it's a little unorthodox how it all unfolded, but plenty of couples work together, and plenty of couples have found their starts here, just like Devon and me."

"Well, those were players. Players are known to be...wild. You're the general manager."

I let out a huff of a laugh. "Well, if it helps you reconcile the situation, I, too, was once a player. So maybe a little of that wild side remains. Frankly, my personal life is really none of your business, and while I appreciate you talking directly to me about it, this discussion is at an end. I'd like you to just get back to your regular work."

She steps toward the door. "I'm sorry, Grant. I didn't mean to offend you. I just hold you in high regard and it felt odd, hearing this news."

Honestly, I can't even bring myself to dignify her with an answer. It makes me feel strange to be judged by my own assistant, and I spend a solid ten minutes after she leaves my office waging an internal debate about whether I should go and tell her she crossed a line with me and if she'd like to keep her job as my assistant, don't fucking cross it again.

It's not like this is the first time I've been the subject of salacious office gossip, unfortunately. When Margot and I ended things, the news spread like wildfire. Particularly the part where I found her naked with my friend and coworker. I was mortified, of course, but I was not viewed as the bad guy in that scenario. This time? Well, we shall see.

I do wonder where the news came from, though. I don't feel that Max would spread rumors around the office. For one, he only comes in for scheduled meetings and team events. Curious, I pop my head out and ask Marielle, "Can I ask the source of the gossip you heard?"

My assistant cringes and looks around as if she's about to give away a state secret. "Well, I heard it from one of the ticketing guys, who says he heard it from one of the players. Apparently, the player is dating Ms. Pearson's friend."

Ah. So that would be Mikhail. Interesting.

"Thank you. You've told me all I need to know."

"For what it's worth," Marielle says. "I'm happy for you, if you're happy."

"I am happy. But I'd like for you to focus on your job here rather than the latest office gossip."

"Yes, of course. I'm so sorry I ever mentioned it at all," Marielle apologizes, quickly realizing she's poked a sleeping bear with her *inquiry*.

I manage to make it through the rest of the day without any more drama, thankfully, but I'm in a foul mood as I head home, a mood made darker when my phone rings, Margot's name on the caller ID.

"What do you need, Margot?" I'm curt, verging on rudeness.

"Wow, frosty reception," she answers. When I don't respond, she says, "I hear you've already knocked up one of your employees. Boy, that wasn't super smart, now, was it?"

"It's literally none of anyone's or your business," I nearly hiss. Goddamn, news travels fast. "And don't be a hypocrite. You got pregnant five minutes after we were through."

Margot lets out a loud sigh on the other end of the line. "Grant, I need to tell you something."

"Oh boy," I mutter. "This ought to be good."

"I never went off the pill when I was with you."

It hits just where she means it to. I feel like I might vomit.

"What?" is all I can muster in answer, and it hardly comes out at all.

"I didn't want kids, Grant. But you did. And you were loud and insistent about it. So I pretended to be willing to try, and I pretended to be upset when my period came each month. Because I figured it would be better to think we were trying, to think it couldn't happen, than to tell you that I just didn't want children."

"Not with me."

"Not at all," she says. "I didn't want them at all.

But you wouldn't listen. You were obsessed with it. So I thought this would be the best. Better than derailing our relationship just because we weren't on the same page about kids."

"So you derailed our relationship by sleeping with my friend, instead?" *Is this bitch for real right now?*

You know, you think you're over a situation, that it's in the past and can't hurt you anymore. And then your ex just totally levels you with some total, manipulative bullshit. My blood absolutely boils.

"It was all about having kids for you," she argues. "You stopped giving a shit about me, about our relationship."

"That is *not* true. I wanted to build on our life together. To build a family."

"You were out of your damn mind about having kids. Nothing else mattered." She's on a rant for some reason, which, thankfully, is not my problem anymore.

"I have apologized. I have told you I was sorry for pushing you, for wanting it so badly. I know I played into the end of what we had. We've already done this, Margot. Why do it again? And why tell me now, that you lied? That you lied to me and let me think you wanted what I wanted? Why do this now? Just to hurt me now that I'm happy?"

"Happy?" Margot scoffs. "Grant, you've knocked up an employee, not found your soulmate."

"How fucking dare you," I snarl. "You lying,

selfish, cheating, cu—bitch." Stopping just short of using the slur that came to mind first, I make sure to tell her the most important thing, "I can't believe I *ever* loved you," before hanging up on her.

I could throw my phone out the window, I'm so angry. How could love turn into hate like this? How could I have loved someone who so clearly didn't love me back? She cheated and manipulated me intentionally. I want nothing more than to go find a gym and throw punches until I can't feel my arms anymore.

THE FIVE-MILE RUN and the hot shower afterward help some, but not nearly enough. I need to see Devon and have a heart-to-heart. Tell her everything that Margot just blindsided me with.

I grab my keys and wallet and start to head out when the doorbell rings. I swing it open, ready to tell whoever it is to fuck off and be on their merry way.

But it's Devon, the precious mother of my unborn children, looking mouthwateringly gorgeous as always, showing up just when I need her the most.

I pull her inside and into my arms, just holding her and breathing in the scent of her hair, her skin, her warmth. I tug her toward the couch, where we end up half sitting, half leaning, but I don't care. I have her in my arms, and that's everything in the world that I need right now. Just the act of having her in my arms will do in the immediate. She allows it, being the generous and loving person she is, and it's a long time before I can bear to let her go.

Finally, she breaks the heavy silence draped around us. "You seem like you really needed that hug."

"You're not wrong, beautiful. I'm really glad you're here because I was just about to head over to your place."

"Why don't you tell me what's going on?"

"Margot called me." Tipping my head back, I pinch the bridge of my nose and stare at the ceiling.

"Always fun getting a call from the ex." I know she's trying to lighten my mood, which is sweet, but she may not feel that way when I tell her the rest of it.

"Yeah, especially when she says she lied for years. She never went off the pill. She lied about trying. She made me think I was—that I couldn't—" I pitch forward and slam my fists on the coffee table. "I'm so sorry, Devon. When the condom broke, I didn't think it was possible to—"

"I know what you thought. And it's not your fault."

"If I'd known…"

"You'd have done what? Grant, condoms break sometimes. And you had no reason to think we should worry. You went full disclosure by telling me it broke in the first place. It's not your fault."

"I thought it was me. She just never really tried at

all. Now this feels like a bigger betrayal than when she cheated on me."

"Look here." Devon reaches out and takes my hand in hers. "We're both better for being away from our exes. They had their own agendas, and those agendas didn't really include us. We're free of all that now, and we found each other. We have two precious babies on the way. I think we both ended up right where we were always meant to be."

I want to be able to tell her that nothing else matters to me because she's totally right. Margot is my past; Devon and the twins are my future. But today has done a number on me. "Everyone knows about us, Dev. They think I'm some gross guy in a position of power who sluts around impregnating the staff."

"How does everyone know?"

"Best I can gather, your friend Gia told Mikhail, who told someone else, and so on. Margot called to tell me even she'd heard the rumor. In *Canada*."

"Oh." Devon's expression goes dark for a moment before she takes a steadying breath and sits up. "Well, people were going to find out somehow. I mean, we weren't subtle that one night after class. Evan already knew, and his wife Holly. Which probably means Pam and Georg knew, and so probably Tyler and Zoya knew. It just works like that. And I'm not embarrassed. I care about you. You care about me. So the gossipers can just fuck off about it. It doesn't matter what others know or even what they think they know."

"You're right." I agree with her, but I'm not ready to shake my mood just yet. Devon, sensing this, crawls to the floor, on her knees, in between my legs. She runs her hands up and down my thighs, up inside one leg of my athletic shorts. A devilish grin on her face, she teases my balls with her fingernails, my cock surging in response to what she's doing to me.

"Listen, Mr. Crankypants, no one said this was going to be easy. But I'm here cooking your babies. And we're together. So quit being so emo."

I tilt my head and try not to smile. "Emo? Seriously?"

"I just call it like I see it, but you know what always makes cranky boys feel better?"

She's got her hand wrapped around the shaft now, stroking me as I close my eyes, getting lost in her touch. She pulls my shorts down, exposing me, touching me until I can hardly stand it. But when I move to kiss her, she shakes her head, still grinning. Her eyebrows quirk mischievously as she dips her head, taking me into her mouth, licking and sucking at the head of my cock. It's a total tease but a good one.

I groan, needing more, and she responds, taking me deeper, deeper, her hand cupping my balls as she sucks. I'm mesmerized, watching her. It's so sexy. I want to tell her, but I'm struck dumb, unable to speak any words. I couldn't even say my own name right now.

I've never seen such a sensual display—one I know she's putting on just to make me feel better. My mind flits from this amazing woman in front of me back to the frustrations of the day. As if she can read into my mind, Devon stops what she's doing and pulls her mouth off my cock. *Busted.*

"I'm sorry—"

"Guess I'll just have to try harder." She smirks and makes a show of stripping off her shirt, slowly pulling it up over her head before freeing her gorgeous tits from the confines of her bra.

I groan at the sight of her, so perfect, her belly with its small swell of our babies growing within, her breasts getting heavier as she goes further into her pregnancy.

"There we go," she says smugly, returning to her project, taking my cock in her hands as she licks from tip to base, her sexy bedroom eyes never leaving mine.

When she sucks me all the way down to the back of her throat, I'm so lost to the erotic sight of her taking my cock and the release I'm about to spill down her throat. When I come in her mouth in the next two seconds, I erupt violently. Shuddering into her, the pleasure is unimaginably good, rolling through my body to the beat of the sexy sounds she makes while swallowing down every last drop.

Fuck me.

I can't believe this beautiful, amazing, loving woman is mine.

When she crawls onto my lap, my hands on her bare back, her head on my shoulder, she whispers, "Still thinking about Margot?"

I laugh out loud. "Margot who?" I vow to never say her name again.

We settle on our sides, spooning on the couch, my hand resting on her bare belly. I press a kiss into the crook of her neck, on the edge of her shoulder, the shell of her ear...until she's softly moaning, turning toward me, offering her lips for more.

"Devon," I tell her between kisses, "I love you. I'm so in love with you. You're the best puck luck that's *ever* happened to me and I just need you to know, right now, this second, just how much I love you."

Her breath catches, and she whispers, "That was some *puck luck* indeed, my love. One really, super-lucky, one-night puc—"

I cut her off with a deep kiss, slipping a hand down into her leggings, finding her warm and wet and ready for me. She grinds against my hand, seeking more of the friction of my touch. Twisting toward me even more, she offers up her own passionate kisses in a rhythm with my fingers stroking so very deeply inside her. The pregnancy hormones make her so responsive these days that I have her coming on my fingers in less than a minute. The soft cries of her climax purposefully stolen with endless, possessive kisses by me. Given the chance, I'll always steal kisses from her because I will never have enough of them.

Wrapped up in one another, half naked and sated, she captures my face in her hands, forcing me to look at her. "My turn," she says with another kiss. "Grantham Gerard, you beautiful, amazing man, I'm so in love with *you*. You're everything I could ever want in a partner to love me, to be the best father ever to our children, to make a life with. I never stood a chance from falling in love with you. You had me from the very first moment, in all honesty, when you walked over to talk to me in that hotel bar. You were my lucky puck that night. So very, very lucky."

All thoughts of the past slip away and just disappear, replaced by the joy of knowing that this woman loves me. She's smart, talented, gorgeous, and so very loving, and I know she'll be the best mother on earth to the precious little humans we made together. She's exactly what I want and everything I never knew I needed. But most of all, she loves me.

"This may sound too soon, but I've been thinking. I have space here. Three bedrooms. We could turn one into a nursery. Save the other for a home office for you. I know it's not a forever home, but we could all live here together to start out while we settle into parenthood and figure out where we want to live..."

I trail off my rushed, rambling invitation to move in here with me as Devon's eyes go wide. I think I've made a mistake and scared her away, but then she's right back to touching my face, forcing me to focus on her beautiful brown eyes. "That's better, my love. Are you worried I'll say no?"

"I know it's fast, but please don't say no." I'm pretty sure I sound desperate as fuck, but who am I kidding? I *am* desperate. For her. Always, I'll need her. "I'll beg if it helps my case."

"It's all been fast, Grant," she says, still touching my face, caressing back and forth across my cheek with her thumb. "No need for begging though, because I love you. I didn't consider myself lonely until I met you. In fact, I quite liked my single life, being able to run when I like, eat what I want. And although those things were great, I've felt this sense of loss...or missing something since, especially after meeting you. The idea of coming home every day to you, or with you, makes me so happy. I really just like being with you as a person, Grant, and I honestly can see myself here with you. Thank you." She puts my hand on her belly. "These babies love you too. Of course, we want to live with you."

32

more than just a
lucky puck

Devon

One month later.

I'm only four months along, but I look more like six months because there are two babies growing like weeds inside of me. I can't even imagine what I'll look like in two or three more months. A flotation device, probably.

When I suggested that to Gia yesterday, she nearly wet her pants from laughing so hard. *Great friend she is.* We had quite the serious heart-to-heart, which was surprising. Naturally, she swooned the first time I told her Grant loved me and wasn't at all shocked. But her words yesterday touched me deeply. *"Dev, I am so incredibly happy for you. You've always been upbeat and fun, and I love that about you. But you are positively glowing now. I had no idea the love of a good man could transform someone, but it has you. And I couldn't be happier. You're going to make the best parents simply because you love each other so selflessly. I'm a little jealous, if I'm honest."* Of course, that made me cry—thank you, pregnancy hormones—which even brought tears to her eyes. I hugged her, hard, and told her she was going to make the best auntie and godmother to our babies. Good lord, there were tears after that too.

I smile as I think about that conversation. And then that smile drops as I tick through hangers in my wardrobe. There are not many professional-looking outfits left that will fit me now. Which sucks because Grant's first preseason press event is tonight, and he really wants me there. Thus far, I have managed to avoid these types of events. The players get all dressed up in suits and their spouses attend, sometimes even their children. The events are meant to give the press personal access to the players and staff, to get their thoughts on the season and to get to know them as humans. It's been a tradition since before I started here, and I've not been invited because, honestly, who wants to get a sound bite from the nutritionist? Snooze.

It's a significant night for Grant though—like a coming-out party as the new GM. And he's made a lot of changes, so I'm sure the members of the press will have a ton of questions. He looks calm and collected as he puts on his tie, not a shred of nervousness showing.

"Ugh. I have nothing to wear. And you look perfect and sexy and fly as hell, to quote a certain admirer from my past. I'm just going to be this big whale in the corner. Maybe I should stay home and invite Gia to come and eat Ben & Jerry's with me and we'll just Netflix and chill. Nobody cares if I'm there or not."

Grant steps over and kisses me on the forehead. "Well, *I* most certainly care if you're there. In fact, I insist on showing you off tonight, making certain everybody knows we are a team. Having you there by my side is the best part of this shindig tonight."

"I'll give you points for all that positive encouragement, but this wardrobe situation of mine is ridiculous. I'm so going shopping this weekend."

"Perfect. I'll go with you. I'll be your personal shopper, bring you stuff to try on, carry all your bags, pay for everything, and I'll even throw in a foot massage when we get home." He gives me a sexy wink and goes right back to his tie as if he's just solved a First World problem.

"You know, Gerard, it's probably illegal for you to be this handsome *and* supportive at the same time, to your hormone-addled baby mama." I give him a playful smack to his ass and return to flicking through the contents of my closet.

"Not when my hormone-addled baby mama is you,

Pearson," he says without missing a beat, still working on his tie.

"Hmm, this could work, maybe." I take out a black wrap dress that looks promising. The style of the dress and fabric are on point, at least. I step into the bathroom and pull it on. It fits okay for the most part, makes my boobs look humongous, and my bump clearly prominent under the fabric belt at my waist. Or what poses for a waist at the moment. It's more like right under my boobs, to be honest. The only part of me below the shoulders that looks normal is my legs, showcased by my favorite Jimmy Choo slingbacks in glittery white gold.

After fussing with my hair and my makeup, I step back out into the bedroom and clear my throat.

Grant wolf whistles. "God, you look mahhhvelous. And fuckin' hot."

"Don't patronize me, Gerard. I really do feel like a whale, and nothing fits right. Imagine how bad this will be in another month or two? I'm going to get huge."

"Well, *Pearson*, as I said earlier, you are always beautiful to me, huge or not. It's *all* fitting right, trust me on this." Pulling me into a hug, he rests his chin on the top of my head. "I've always wanted to have a beach ball between us while we're having sex. Total fantasy of mine."

I can't help but laugh at the image it creates. "That sounds so...hot."

"Everything is hot with you. Please know that I'll happily have sex with you, regardless of how *huge* you get."

"Well, there will come a time when you'll forget what I look like because we'll only be able to do it from behind," I joke, feeling lighter already, just knowing he still finds me desirable.

"Mmm," he grumbles in my ear, nibbling at the lobe as his hand snakes up the back of my dress, dipping into the space between my legs. "We could do fun things from behind."

I shoo him away. "No thank you. You're not going to get me all hot and bothered now. I don't need one more reason to be uncomfortable at this event."

"Good, I want you hot and bothered," he says, giving me a wolf's grin. "I only want you thinking about me tonight."

He really is too handsome for his own good. Every woman in the joint (and probably a few of the men) will be "thinking" about him tonight. "Well, how about you *and* dessert?"

He laughs softly, rolling his lips together. "That'll do, beautiful, me and dessert it is then."

AS SOON AS we're spotted on the gold carpet, Grant is immediately steered toward the press throng as I scan the gathering for familiar faces. Pam and

Holly are talking away from the crowd, so I make a beeline over to them. As I get close, I hear Holly saying something about how sad it is that a press event poses for a date night lately.

"You had a date night at my class recently," I say, joining their conversation.

Pam's eyes light up as she touches my baby bump. "I know, I know, you're not supposed to touch a pregnant woman's belly, but yours is so freaking cute!"

"Welcome to the club of fraternizers," Scarlett says as she joins our group, making us all laugh. "And you do look awfully cute pregnant. I felt disgusting the whole time I was pregnant the first time, and only marginally less so this time."

"Everyone feels disgusting when they're pregnant," Holly says.

"Well, I've got two buns in this oven, so I'm guessing I'll win the argument over who feels bigger and more hideous by the end."

"You're perfect," Pam says, grinning. "You'll probably look perfect all the way to the end. Like, you'll still have your perfect, toned arms and your perfect, skinny legs, and there'll just be this perfect little ball of a stomach in between. And amazing tits. Let's not forget those, not that we could with the way they're taking a starring role in that dress."

We all laugh again as I lament my issues getting dressed, the fact that my bras don't fit, and my total lack of motivation regarding exercise these past months.

"If you need someone to jog with, I'm always out with the running stroller," Holly offers.

"Ugh, not me. Exercise is not my thing, nor will it ever be," Scarlett adds.

I've always liked these women, but it does feel different now, being part of a secret club. Or not-so-secret, I suppose. "So, you and Grant met before he started here?" Scarlett asks.

"We did. He had just gotten the job offer, and I was at his hotel for a conference. We made a pact to not talk about work or exes."

"I imagine there wasn't much talking at all," Pam says, raising her eyebrows suggestively. "I mean, just look at the man."

"Look at the *woman*," Holly says with a laugh. "Christ, those are going to be some good-looking babies."

I blush, but the conversation is halted as the event starts. Max Terry kicks things off, noting that he usually skips these preseason press events, but he wanted to be here in person to introduce the team's new general manager.

"He's made some changes that I fully support, and which I believe will take our team into its next metamorphosis. We have been at the top. But to stay there, we need vision and innovation in the way we think about coaching, playing, and managing a team. I have total faith in Grant Gerard's leadership."

After a thundering applause of introduction, Grant takes the mic and launches into his prepared statement. He talks about coming from a player's background, about understanding the game in a way some administrators don't. He thanks the coaches and players for embracing his ideas and changes, and he talks about what those changes have been.

The press ask him a ton of questions, and he handles everything like the total pro that he is. After about ten minutes, Max jumps in and says, "I'm sure you're all eager to chat with your favorite players, so let's just do one more question for Grant and then open it up to the team."

"Are you happy you made the move?" someone asks.

Grant gives a dazzling smile that sets off plenty of camera flashes and nearly melts my maternity panties. As if I wasn't already hot and bothered from our earlier dalliance.

"I am. I needed this change, both personally and professionally. I needed a challenge and I needed to grow. This has provided everything I could have asked for, and more. It feels like it was meant to be. I'm super stoked to see what the season brings, but I do have one loose end I need to tie up tonight if you'll all indulge me for just a moment."

So gorgeous in his charcoal silk suit and his tie in

bright gold, he steps out from behind the podium. Taking just a few, long strides, he drops down to one knee in front of me. I suck in an audible breath, my hand coming up to my mouth in surprise.

"Devon Josephine Pearson, we got the timeline a little muddled up here, but it's only forward from this point on. You are my favorite thing about Las Vegas— you have been since the day I interviewed for my job here. And I can't wait to be parents together. But first, I want to be more than just a really lucky puck for you. I love you so very much, and I want to be your husband. Your partner. Your biggest supporter. Devon, will you marry me?"

Popping open a ring box, he presents me with a sparkling emerald-cut solitaire. I can clearly hear all the sighs from people throughout the room, but I can't see much of anything because I'm totally crying. If you'd told me twelve months ago I'd be pregnant and receiving a marriage proposal a year later, I would have said you were out of your damn mind. But life has a funny way of changing in miraculous ways. This next twelve months is going to bring about even more incredible changes. There is only one answer for this ridiculously handsome, wonderfully supportive man down on one knee before me. "Yes. I'd love to marry you, Grantham Gerard."

Everyone cheers and claps and whoops as he stands and puts the engagement ring on my finger, pulling me into his arms for a kiss.

"Christ, it would've been so embarrassing if you'd said no," he says into my ear. "But I heard this team likes these moments to be big, so…"

"Well, that was pretty big, and also pretty perfect, my supremely hot and oh so lucky puck." I kiss my husband-to-be on the lips in front of everybody. "Like I would ever say no to the man I'm spending the rest of my life with," I whisper back to him.

33

sharing joys and pains

Grant

Three weeks later.

We just won our home opener by a huge margin—five to one, with a second-string forward scoring two of those goals. We played a more comprehensive game, with more subs than usual, and I'm thrilled to see the work we've done paying off.

At the post-game press conference, Coach Brown talks about the effort to prepare the next generation of Crush winners by having them play more minutes. Evan jumps in and heads off the inevitable question about whether or not the starters are miffed about not getting the usual amount of playing time, telling the media types that these are all professionals who are all on the team for a reason. The team is not one individual person or even a line of players. He does a nice job of supporting the second- and third-string players while still assuring the public that they'll see plenty of their favorite players on the ice this season.

Devon waits at the back of the room, nursing a glass of seltzer water. She looks amazing in a Crush sweater and denim leggings, the swell of her belly prominently bigger than when I proposed to her at the season opening presser. I can't get enough of looking at her, honestly. She thinks she looks hideous, but all I see is a beautiful woman lovingly growing our babies. What could be sexier?

As things wrap up, I congratulate the guys and head out, my hand on Devon's back as I usher her to a side entrance, where a sleek, black limousine awaits.

Devon looks at me with some confusion. "I don't recall it being prom night. Otherwise, I'd have worn something much more sparkly."

I laugh as we slide in, side by side, on the leather seat. "Trust me." I take her left hand in mine and bring it up to my lips for a kiss, her diamond ring winking at me at eye level.

We talk about the game as we ride along, and when we finally stop, and the door opens, Devon bursts into laughter. We are stopped in front of a cheesy Las Vegas wedding chapel. "Really?" she asks, still laughing. I hold both of her hands as we stand outside the doors, the foot traffic of tourist Vegas moving around us as if we don't exist. "Look, I don't want to wait, Devon. I want to be your husband. We can plan something more traditional after the babies are born for our families and friends to celebrate with us, but the event is not as important to me as the act of making us husband and wife. And I don't see any reason to wait."

"Well, I might've worn something other than Vans and stretchy jeans." Devon looks somewhat shell-shocked, but I sense happiness, too, which is good for me.

"I think you look perfect. You look like the woman I love. My gorgeous baby mama who I'd love to make my wife if you'll let me."

She looks at the door, then at me, then at the door again. "Okay. Let's do it."

With a hoot of celebration, I usher her inside, where a staff member greets us. "Congrats on the win tonight," she says, eyeing Devon's Crush sweater. "And welcome to the Little Chapel of the Desert. You have a choice of who will marry you tonight. Elvis, Jerry Garcia, or Wonder Woman. Any preference from those three?"

We both look at each other and say at the same time, "Wonder Woman."

We're led back into the chapel, where we watch another couple get married by a bearded man who looks only slightly like Jerry Garcia. Devon laughs silently beside me the whole time. When it's our turn, we head up to the altar, joined by a passable Wonder Woman, who looks more like the original than the current. Still, when she talks about building a partnership, about finding someone who allows you to be yourself, about finding someone you can share your joys and pains with—well, we both get a little emotional.

After our I do's are finished, I kiss her more voraciously than is probably appropriate in public. Devon Pearson Gerard is now my wife.

When I came here for my interview, I was seeking an escape, a new challenge, a way to move beyond my past. What I found was a home and the rest of my life with a partner who loves me and who is giving us a beautiful family.

I'm the luckiest fuckin' *puck* of all.

BACK IN THE LIMO, Devon hits the button to separate the driver from the back end of the car before pulling off her shoes, and then her jeans, and lastly, her underwear. "Look at you, Mrs. Gerard, gettin' your sexy on." She ignores me, her fingers going for my pants and unbuttoning them instead, freeing my hardening cock from my boxers. She's on me like an animal, her pussy wet and ready to be fucked as my wife for the first time. I help her to get into position to straddle me as we kiss more hungrily, the need to connect physically overtaking everything else.

Touching Devon's belly, now protruding as her sweater rides up, I whisper, "Cover your eyes, kids," and she smacks me playfully.

"All that talk about partnership and sharing your joys and pains," she says as she starts to ride me. "I didn't expect to feel so...moved."

"Moved to sex me up in the back of a limousine," I growl as I pull her jersey over her head and bury my face in the warmth of her now even more spectacular tits. "Let's get married every day."

She moves on top of me like her life depends on it, until her pussy clenches and her head flops backward, her breath stopping. I hold her hips, enjoying the wave of her orgasm until she comes back to reality, moving again, even faster this time.

"I would," she says, breathless. "I love you so much. I'd marry you every day."

That's it. I lose myself in her, pulling her close, my face at her neck as I come.

"Oh my God," Devon says as we both try to catch our breath. "That was..."

"Yeah, this woman I just married must truly love me to do all that in the back of a moving vehicle."

"Mm-hmm." She climbs off me, pulling her clothing back on and sorting herself out, the whole time looking very pleased with herself, grinning like a Cheshire cat.

I can only think again about how lucky I am.

Soon after, the limo stops in front of the home we now share together. Our first home together, but certainly not the last. We'll need more room for the kids as they grow, for sure. I'll want a big backyard with a pool and a basketball court, and Devon wants to start a culinary greenhouse. Plants have to be protected more from the heat than the cold to grow well in the desert, so we need a large property, also a place to park her silver Ford F150 farm truck. I haven't forgotten her dream car. We'd like to have a home gym for boxing and yoga, and even a test kitchen for Devon's business once she gets that rolled out. Step by step, of course, but big plans are in the works for the Gerards of Las Vegas. It has been so mind-blowing planning these things with Devon. From the start, our thoughts and desires aligned so easily, something I know now I never really had with my ex (she who shall not be named). Devon and I just work...like a team. We're both thoughtful of each other's needs and wants, and it's an extraordinary thing. *She is my forever, which is abundantly clear.*

We stumble out of the car, holding hands, running for the front door. I unlock it and make a big show of picking up my wife to carry her over the threshold. She squeals and swats at me, telling me she's an elephant, too heavy for me to carry. I pay her no attention, kissing her protests away as we step inside.

"What now?" I ask.

"I don't know. We're a boring married couple now. I guess I'll work on book edits and you can, like, watch highlight reels?"

I have to stifle my laugh. "I think I have a better idea." I kiss my new wife while carrying her down the hall. "Bedroom, Mrs. Gerard."

epilogue

Devon

Four months later.

"I love you so much, babe. You're so beautiful to me right now."

I let out a groan of pain, trying to remember the breathing exercises I learned in the childbirth class we took together. And I know Grant's job is to be supportive and calm, but if he says I look beautiful one more time, I'm gonna snap and transform this hospital room into a scene from *The Exorcist*, sending all these people fleeing for their friggin lives. "Beautiful" will be the last word he'll dream of using to describe me then.

"Okay, Devon," Dr. Reilly says, "it's time to push. On your next contraction, bear down and count with me."

I nod as Grant feeds me an ice chip. As another

contraction starts, Dr. Reilly signals me to bear down. He counts, starting at ten, as I grit my teeth through the intense pain.

"Almost there," Dr. Reilly soothes. "I see the first head. Which one will it be? This twin is forever the older of the two. The other will always be *little* brother or sister."

Another contraction levels me and I cry out, pushing as hard as I can as Dr. Reilly counts again. A short tear of pain is followed by a moment of relief.

"Baby number one is a boy!" he announces.

"Nathan," Grant says. "His name is Nathan." We're calling him Nate after Grant's beloved Grandpa Nate, who was at every hockey practice without fail when he was just starting out as a little boy learning the game.

I have no time to revel in the birth of my first child. The nurses carry him over to a scale, weighing him, cleaning him off, and checking his vitals, all as another round of contractions start up. Doc tells me not to push yet. We wait through two more contractions before he gives me a, "Go."

A minute later, my daughter is born. "Josephine," Grant says without ever taking his eyes off her. Named after my sweet grandma, who I know is smiling down on us all right now from heaven.

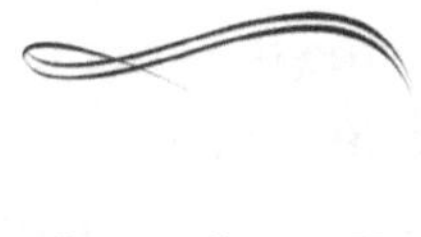

IT'S another few hours before we're alone in our room. We sent Grant's mom and dad home a while ago. They're over the moon at the birth of their first grandbabies and are staying in town to help us out these first few weeks for those round-the-clock feedings I've heard so much about. Auntie Gia was next to head out with so many kisses and hugs, and trailing more balloons and baby toys and booties behind her than the hospital gift shop could've had in stock. It must be bare shelves in there after she stopped in. She's going to take some vacation time and also help me out during this first week. I'm so blessed to have all this support right at the beginning, until we all get settled into our groove.

I look over at Grant holding Josie while I work on learning how to nurse Nate. They're ridiculously beautiful little people, though I might be a tad biased. And I'm so tired, but I can't stop looking at them, can't stop thinking about how right this feels. We are a family of four now, and this is so far beyond what I imagined for myself even a year ago, or ever, really.

"Can you believe these two?" The awe sounding in Grant's voice is so clear, so strong. He hasn't stopped smiling since they were born. "They are, by far, the cutest babies I have ever seen."

"I just had the same thought." I grin, bopping our son's tiny little nose with my pinky finger. "We need to call Brett. Can't imagine the grief he'll give me if I wait to tell *my* big brother that I'm a mom. That his nephew and niece are here." Grant chuckles and gets his phone out of his pocket.

I'm a mom. And I've been blessed with two gorgeous and perfect little babies. It's moments like these that I miss my grandma and wish she could be here to see them. To hold her great-grandchildren. Wishing she could be here to give me advice on how to mother two at one time. *And, when the time comes, juggle my new business.*

I grimace slightly. "I'm so nervous about leaving the Crush. No idea why that thought just passed through my mind. I just gave birth mere hours ago. But it's almost as though this is the day I've been waiting for and it's finally here. And now my new life really starts."

"I can understand that, but you'll be amazing. Give yourself time to adapt to being a mom first, yeah?"

"God, yes. Must be the extra hormones. My mind is spinning." Holly's been so helpful with suggestions, and I know in my heart it'll all work out as it's supposed to. Just...a little scary. Leaving something that's a sure thing. Taking a risk like this. Especially with these two precious people to care for. Maybe my plans do change, who knows? I just know this is a ridiculous time to be making decisions about my career path. Right now, I have the only job I want cuddled in my arms and in my husband's. *Good. Glad that's settled.*

Grant leans over and kisses me gently on the lips.

"When the time comes to launch Fit 2 Cook, you'll know it, and you'll have the opportunity to be doing something else you love."

"And I've got a smart, sexy, supportive husband with a swanky job that has benefits." I send him an air kiss since both of us have our hands full with babies.

"This, too, is true."

"Is she out yet?" I ask about our daughter in his arms.

"Sleeping like the dead." Grant stands slowly, carefully placing Josie in the nearby bassinet the hospital has in my room. He turns his back to me for a moment while he roots around in the gym bag he hastily packed as we were freaking out when my contractions started. When he turns, he holds out a jewelry box, flipping it open to reveal an amazing pair of emerald-cut diamond earrings matched to my wedding ring.

"Oh, my love, they're stunning. You didn't have to."

"I know," Grant says softly. "But you are everything to me. Our kids are everything to me. And I wanted to find something to show you, even in this inadequate way, how precious you are. Beautiful children you've given to me, just like yourself, but it's all of this. It's so much more than beauty. It's the whole of you, Devon. It's your heart. Your personality. Your focus. Your creativity. You are perfect in my eyes, many times more perfect than these gemstones."

I start crying. Not prettily either. I'm full-on ugly crying, the reality of this full picture coming into focus. I've found someone who appreciates and loves me and who supports me. I have these two beautiful children now, making us a family of four. All I can manage, though, is, "I didn't get you anything."

Grant laughs, his own eyes shining as he leans in and kisses my temple.

"Wrong. You gave me everything."

my thoughts about...

afterword

Extensive creative license was applied in portraying some elements of NHL games, fan events and awards, that would ***not happen in real life***. I did this intentionally to create a more enjoyable reading experience within the storyline. These stories have been carefully crafted for your reading pleasure and in no way meant to be a true and accurate representation of NHL best practices and/or official rules currently or in the past.

Hockey Romance F-I-C-T-I-O-N all the way!!!

vegas crush by trope

All books in the *VEGAS CRUSH* series are *STANDALONES* existing in a connected world centering around a Las Vegas ice-hockey team. You can read them out of order if you wish and everything will still make sense with only minor spoilers. I've made a list of tropes for you here.

CRUSHED

BOOK 1

Forbidden, Reformed "Player", Ukrainian/American Hero, Good Girl Heroine, Office Romance, Love in the Workplace, He Falls First, Sports Romance, Team Captain, Social Media Manager, Risking it All for Love, Band of Brothers

BOOK 2

Bad Boy Russian Hero, Virgin Heroine, Damaged Heroine, Forbidden, Office Romance, Hockey Defenseman, Team Physical Therapist, Love in the Workplace, Band of Brothers, Overcoming Self-Doubt and Addiction, Trust

Red ROCKET

BOOK 3

Grumpy/Sunshine, Russian Hero, Feisty Red-Haired Heroine, Forbidden, Office Romance, Hockey Defenseman, Public Relations Manager, Love in the Workplace, He Falls First, Brooding Alpha, Opposites Attract, Band of Brothers

Puck MONEY

BOOK 4

Opposites Attract, Forbidden Romance, Financial Advisor/Client Relationship, Russian/Romanian Hero, Nerdy Young Heroine, Fresh Start in Vegas, Dyslexic Hero, Gentleman Alpha, Good Guy Hero, He Falls First, Age Gap, Vegas Mafia Suspense, Savior Hero, Band of Brothers, Superstar Hockey Centerman

BOOK 5

Friends to Lovers, Teammates Little Sister, Young Virgin Heroine, Russian Heroine, Boston Native, Bad Boy Hero, Forbidden Romance, First Love, Age Gap, Single "Dad" Vibes, Hardscrabble Upbringing, Band of Brothers, Hockey Defenseman, New Adulting, Found Family

BOOK 6

Enemies to Lovers, Forced Proximity, Love in the Workplace, Neuro-Diverse Hero, French-Canadian Hero, Rock Chick Heroine, Socially Awkward w/ No Filter, Opposites Attract, Instant Attraction, Fish Out of Water, Band of Brothers, Superstar Hockey Goalie, Rockstar Heroine, Brooding Alpha, Guitar Lessons w/ Cute Kids, Personal Growth, Sacrificing for Love

Lucky PUCK

BOOK 7

Surprise Pregnancy, One Night Stand, Forbidden Romance, Love in the Workplace, Boss/Employee, Office Romance, Sneaky Dates, Instant Attraction, Age Gap, Mature Hero, Gentleman Alpha, Love After Divorce, Can't Keep Their Hands off Each Other, Career Milestones, Team General Manager, Team Nutritionist

Mr. HOCKEY

BOOK 8

Friends With Benefits, Instant Attraction, He Falls First, Brooding Alpha, Superhero Complex, Gentleman Alpha, Damsel in Distress, Knight in Shining Armor, Living up to Father's Legacy, Vegas Mafia Suspense, Comic Book Nerd, Wedding Planner Heroine, Band of Brothers, Finding Your Voice, Parent/Child Relationships

BOOK 9

Age Gap, Secret Crush, Surprise Pregnancy, Shotgun Wedding, Opposites Attract, The Owner's Granddaughter, The Brooding Hockey Player, Forced Proximity, Only 1 Bed, Career Milestones, Forbidden, Old Family Friends, *Neanderthal* Hero, *Heiress* Heroine, Parenthood, Beliefs, Growing Up, Manning Up, Facing Your Demons, Family Legacy

BOOK 10

Christmas Marriage Proposal, No Third-Act Breakup, Proposal Problems, Brooding Hockey Player Hero, Buying a Home, Festive Holidays, Dear Santa Letter, Gentleman Alpha, Building a Legacy, Comic Book Nerd, Wedding Planner Heroine, Team Captain, Band of Brothers, Family Relationships, OTT Romantic Gifts

about the author

BRIT DEMILLE is the alter ego of *NYT* Bestselling author, Raine Miller, having an absolute blast writing books quite different from what she writes as Raine.

Stories about sexy billionaires [millionaires make the cut too] who fall in instalove with young women who may or may not be virgins, and then go on to make adorable babies together are her favorite themes. In addition to the billionaires, hot hockey players are at the top of her list of favorite heroes, along with royals and ex-military bodyguards.

Most important when she writes a story is a happily ever after. But during the actual *writing* of the story, the most important thing is a cup of hot tea with a splash of milk (and don't forget the stash of cherry Jolly Ranchers). A dog or two will likely be in between her and the chair at any given moment, which is very handy, because they are the ones who approve everything she writes.

RAINE MILLER is a #2 *New York Times*, *USA Today*, and *Wall Street Journal* bestselling author since 2012. Before that, she spent two decades teaching kiddos to read—something she's most proud of. These days, writing steamy romance books pretty much fills up the hours...for which she keeps pinching herself to make absolutely sure she's not dreaming.

#Truth

She has a handsome husband, two amazing sons, and two very bouncy Italian greyhounds to keep her busy the rest of the time. Her boys know she writes romance books but gratefully they have zero interest in reading even a single one. *Thank. God.*

When she's not writing she's likely deep into a hockey game cheering on her beloved *VEGAS GOLDEN KNIGHTS* and dreaming up a new book. The greyhounds are likely to be in her lap while she writes the books or watches hockey—both dogs at the same time of course!

She loves to hear from readers and chat about the characters she's created.

You can connect with Raine on Facebook in her reader group, **Raine Miller Romance Readers.** She pops in to visit most days because it's a super happy place where romance awesomeness abounds day in and day out with the most amazing readers on earth.

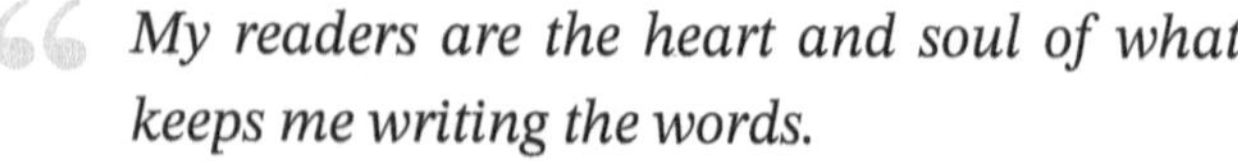

My readers are the heart and soul of what keeps me writing the words.

also by raine miller

The BLACKSTONE AFFAIR

NAKED, Part 1

ALL IN, Part 2

EYES WIDE OPEN, Part 3

RARE and PRECIOUS THINGS, Part 4

The ROTHVALE LEGACY

PRICELESS, I

MY LORD, II

BLACKSTONE DYNASTY

FILTHY RICH, I

FILTHY LIES, II

HOCKEY ROMANCE *as Brit DeMille*

CRUSHED, Vegas Crush #1

SIN SHOT, Vegas Crush #2

RED ROCKET, Vegas Crush #3

PUCK MONEY, Vegas Crush #4

SMOKESHOW, Vegas Crush #5

The KEEPER, Vegas Crush #6

LUCKY PUCK, Vegas Crush #7

Mr. HOCKEY, Vegas Crush #8

CLUSTERPUCK, Vegas Crush #9

Mr. HOCKEY's MARRY CHRISTMAS, Vegas Crush #10

CONTEMPORARY ROMANCE

CHERRY GIRL

HUSBAND MATERIAL

LOVELY PINK

HISTORICAL ROMANCE

The MUSE

The PASSION of DARIUS

The UNDOING of a LIBERTINE

Wedding Night Diaries

LORD BLACKWOOD'S VIRGIN

join raine mail

FOR MY NEWSLETTER and information on upcoming books and events, you should definitely sign up for Raine Mail. Use the QR code below.

whispers *There's so many freebies in that thing.*

subscribe to Raine Mail